REDEEMING THE ROUGHNECKS

BIG G RANCH - BOOK 4

ISABELLA KOLE

SHERI LYNN

Published by Blushing Books
An Imprint of
ABCD Graphics and Design, Inc.
A Virginia Corporation
977 Seminole Trail #233
Charlottesville, VA 22901

Isabella Kole and Sheri Lynn
Redeeming the Roughnecks

Print ISBN: 978-1-63954-111-9
v1

CHAPTER 1

RACHEL

*R*achel Linton wiped an imaginary speck of dust off the skirt of her dress and sighed. What was she doing here, on this train, headed to an uncivilized place called Oklahoma? Her entire family had lost their minds. It had all started with her older sister, Sarah. She loved her sister, but honestly, who goes out west to marry a man she has never met? Mail order bride, indeed! Sarah could have had her pick of the wealthiest men in the east, but no, she didn't want them. She had gotten on a train bound for nowhere, or so Oklahoma seemed to Rachel. She'd married the man she went there for, too. He was a rancher, of all things. Of course, Sarah would never have let her parents think she'd made the biggest mistake of her life. Her letters were always full of praise for her man, love of the place they owned, and talk of the friends she'd made there. Maybe it was true, but to Rachel, she could not imagine such a life making anyone happy. Sarah was different, though. She liked things simple. That was the difference between the two sisters. And

1

when the love of Sarah's life was killed in some sort of accident, one would have thought the girl would have been smart enough to take the next train east, to go home. But no, not Sarah. What did she do? Got herself hitched to another man out there. At least this one was from the east and was a proper businessman.

And that's when their parents had made the horrifying decision to sell everything and move out there to be near Sarah and any grandchildren that might come along, taking Rachel with them. She'd been given no choice, really. Her father had laid down the law. Her life was ruined. She'd be damned if she'd succumb to the charms of one of those western heathens. She was not her sister. So, her plan was to cause so much trouble and aggravation that her parents would quickly send her back home to live with her aunt. She would go back to attending social events and would eventually marry one of the many men who wanted to court her, like any normal, civilized girl would do. Of course, she would have her fun first. No need to rush anything. Marriage could wait.

Rachel loved the social scene, the teas, the balls, dancing until midnight with every available young man and a few who weren't. All that was gone now, thanks to big sister, Sarah.

She would have been agreeable to an extended holiday with her sister and her new family, but to live in that godforsaken place? What were her parents thinking? Who sells everything to pull up stakes and move across the country like that?

Well, she would soon be on a train bound right back to Pennsylvania. She would make sure of that.

To her mother, she said, "How many more days must we be subjected to this train?"

They were sitting in the private car that was theirs for the trip. It had two bedrooms and a small sitting room. Her mother was doing embroidery work, some sort of gift for Sarah, and Rachel was pretending to read.

Mrs. Linton looked up and smiled. "Now, dear, you know it

will be several more days before we reach Sarah and Conrad. We must make the best of it and fill our time as best we can."

Just then, Rachel's father entered the car with two cups of tea. "I thought you girls might be ready for some refreshment," he said as he set the cups down on the table.

"Did you enjoy your cigar and brandy with the men?" his wife asked.

"Yes, indeed. There are a few men on the train who are very interesting to chat with. The smoking car was full."

"That's nice, dear. Rachel is getting restless. Do you know when we will stop again so she can stretch her legs?"

Mr. Linton sighed. "In a few hours. Surely, you can amuse yourself until then." He looked at his younger, difficult daughter.

"Well, if you would allow me to leave this car, I might."

"You know it is much safer for you to remain here unless your mother or I are with you. We have discussed this many times."

"Sarah made the trip alone," Rachel argued.

"Sarah is not you, my sweet daughter," he replied with a chuckle.

Rachel rolled her eyes and went back to her book. Yes, it was true. Sarah and she were two completely different girls.

For the next few hours, she tried to concentrate on the words on the pages of the book. Finally, it was time for a break, and she couldn't wait to get out of the train. They would dine in a real restaurant at least, before re-boarding the train.

When she stepped off and saw the general store/restaurant looming within walking distance, her face fell. Far from what she was used to in the east, she resigned herself to taking her evening meal in the countrified establishment.

"Come, dear, let's look around the store while your father gets a table for us," her mother said as she stepped up beside her.

"How can you be so cheery about this? Do you not realize

that father is moving us to some godforsaken place? Just look at this place. I am sure Oklahoma is even worse than this place."

"Oh, Rachel, where is your sense of adventure? I am sure it will be fine. Your sister certainly has acclimated well."

"I am not my sister. I wish you would all recognize that fact!" she said a little too loudly. Several people turned to stare in their direction.

"Shh, Rachel, you are drawing attention," her mother said.

She rolled her eyes and walked away to look at a rack of ready-made dresses. Who would actually buy a dress off the rack in a general store, anyway? Disgusted, she wondered just how low her sister had fallen since moving out west. At least now, she was married to a businessman. Hopefully, that had restored some class to the rancher's wife Sarah had once been. She was sure Johnny was handsome and all, but a rancher, really?

"Come, our table is ready," Mr. Linton said as he approached his wife and daughter, oblivious to the latest outburst from his youngest.

"Thank goodness!" her mother exclaimed as she took Rachel's arm and pulled her along.

Mr. Linton gave her a funny look, not understanding his wife's impatience, and led them to the table. Then he explained that they would have a guest at their table. "Mr. Thomas, a young man I met on the train, was going to dine alone, so I invited him to join us."

Of course, he did, Rachel thought. *Finally, a normal dinner at a real table and we have to entertain some guy he met on the train.*

Her dad led them to the table where a dark-haired man stood when he saw them approaching. He wasn't bad looking, she supposed. Tall, young, with a mustache and goatee, he looked like he could be from the east, but he was not dressed as such. What was his story?

They all sat down, and the waitress took their drink order and left them menus to look over.

"It will be nice to have a good meal. Not that the food on the train isn't good, but there is something to be said for sitting at a proper table," Mr. Thomas commented as he perused the choices before him.

"I agree," Mr. Linton said. "It's also good to be able to stretch our legs. The next time we stop, we'll be able to sleep in a real bed as well. We will spend the night in a hotel. I'm sorry, I didn't make the introductions. Joshua Thomas, this is my wife, Rosella, and my daughter, Rachel."

"It's so nice to meet you," Mrs. Linton said.

"I'm happy to make your acquaintance as well," the young man replied. He turned to Rachel then. "Miss Linton." He nodded.

"Tell me, Mr. Thomas, where are you from?" Rachel asked.

He chuckled. "I grew up outside of Philadelphia. However, for the last few years I've been in Oklahoma."

"Why on earth?" she asked, to the horror of her parents.

"Rachel!" her father admonished.

"It's quite all right, sir. It isn't like I haven't heard it before from my own family." He laughed and then looked back at Rachel. "To answer your question, though, Miss Linton, I went out west for a change of scenery. I felt stifled working in my father's business. I wanted to explore the world before I settle down to that kind of life. So, I went out west and I've been working on a ranch for the past few years. I am returning from a visit home because of the death of my grandfather."

"And yet you are going back out west," she commented.

Again, he chuckled. "Yes, much to the chagrin of my family, I must say. I found that I like the town I have been living in, and the people. It's more to my liking and I most likely will settle there. When I return, I am to start working for a new oil company. The brother-in-law of one of my employers on the ranch started it, and he needs help."

"That's interesting," Mr. Linton said. "Our older daughter's new husband owns an oil company. His brothers-in-law own the Big G Ranch. Have you heard of it?"

Joshua's eyes grew large. "Heard of it? I worked for the Garrison brothers on the Big G. The oil company I am now going to be working for is Conrad Appleby's. Is he by chance your son-in-law?"

"What a small world," Mrs. Linton said. "Conrad is indeed our son-in-law. We are moving to Oklahoma to be near our daughter, Sarah, and her husband, Conrad."

"Is that right? That's amazing. I had no idea," Joshua said. "So, it looks like we'll be seeing each other on a more permanent basis. Let me be the first to welcome you."

"Why, thank you, Joshua. That is very sweet," Rosella said in response.

"Yes, this is good news indeed. I'm sure you'll make a fine employee for Conrad's company," Mr. Linton said.

Rachel was silent, so Joshua looked over at her and offered, "Miss Linton, I would be happy to show you around when you are settled in your new home."

"Thank you. We shall see," was her non-committal answer.

Her parents gave each other the look they always shared when they were exasperated with their younger daughter. Mr. Thomas, however, took the brush off in stride.

"Very well," he said.

Their meal arrived then, which Rachel was glad of. Imagine, this arrogant man thinking he could make an advance on her. Why on God's green earth would she want a man who had given up the life of an eastern businessman to settle in that no man's land? The nerve of him to even think she would.

Soon, it was time to get back onboard the train. Rachel purchased some peppermint sticks to snack on and immediately went back to her family's private car so she wouldn't have to tell Mr. Thomas no if he asked her to sit with him. The farther away she could be from that man, the better. And the sad thing about it was if she had met him when he lived in Philadelphia, she would have definitely been drawn to his good looks and suave voice. As it was, he was about as deranged as her dear sweet sister. What was it about Oklahoma that drew well-bred easterners to decide to stay there? Well, she would not be one of them. The first chance she got, she would be right back on this awful train, bound for her aunt's house in Philadelphia. She would make sure of that.

~

MR. LINTON WHISPERED to his wife, "You join Rachel in our car. I want to have a word with young Joshua, apologize to him for Rachel's behavior."

"All right, dear, but one of these days, we have to stop doing that and let her face the consequences of her own actions. Joshua seems like such a nice boy, though, so you go on."

He walked her to the door of their car, planted a kiss on her forehead and told her he would see her later. Then he found Joshua and invited him to join him for a cigar and brandy in the smoking car.

"Thank you, sir. I was just heading that way," the young man said.

Once they were comfortably seated, each with a glass of brandy and a cigar, Mr. Linton began, "I must apologize for my daughter. You have to understand that she is not happy about this move. If she'd had her way, she would have remained in Philadelphia with my sister. Part of the reason we are going west to join our other daughter is because we feel Rachel needs a change of scenery. She is a difficult girl, nothing like her older sister, Sarah."

Joshua smiled in understanding. "That does not surprise me. Most eastern girls would balk at the idea. I was not offended. Your older daughter, she likes Oklahoma?"

"Oh my, yes. She made the decision to become a mail order bride a few years ago. Of course, at first we were stunned, but she made it clear that she was not going to settle for any of the young men who had been trying to court her and that she wanted to live a different life. We finally agreed, and she has been in love with the area she settled in ever since she arrived there. Her first husband, a rancher, was killed in an accident. We wanted to come out then, but there was the house to sell, things to settle, and well, it just didn't happen. When she recently remarried, we decided not to put it off any longer. We sold our house and some of the furnishings with it. What we wished to keep will be sent out when we find a home. Luckily, she had some good friends who took her in and helped her during her mourning period. We had thought she might come home then, but she didn't."

"I believe I know who she is. The Garrisons are the ones who took her in. She's a pretty thing, very sweet from what I know of her."

"Yes, yes, it was Clayton and Clara Mae Garrison. Conrad Appleby is Mrs. Garrison's brother."

Joshua nodded and took a drink of his brandy. "Tell me about Rachel. You say she is difficult. Maybe she hasn't yet met the man who can tame her."

At that remark, Mr. Linton chuckled. "I don't know that there is a man alive who can tame that one. I certainly haven't been able to."

"The right man will."

Mr. Linton looked at Joshua through new eyes. "Well, let me just say that my younger daughter enjoys partying, flirting, leading men on, with no intention of settling down with any of them. We feared for her reputation, and thus, the move."

"Ah, I see. Well, living in Oklahoma will be a new experience for her. The folks there are right neighborly and friendly, but the men are looking to settle down if they haven't already. With her

8

pretty, fair hair and skin, she will have them all wishing to court her."

"Pardon my saying this, but they will not stick around long once her snobbish eastern ways make themselves known."

"All the more reason she needs the right man."

"Am I correct in believing that you think you might be that man?" Mr. Linton asked.

"You are, indeed, sir. I would ask your permission to court her, but I think the lady has made it quite clear she is not exactly excited by that thought."

"Give it some time, son. Let her get settled, get to know her ways, and then if you still feel the same way, we'll talk again. I agree that she needs a dominant man who can handle her the right way yet give her plenty of love and attention."

The two men, having reached an understanding, enjoyed the rest of their cigars and brandy before saying goodnight. Joshua returned to his car and Mr. Linton to his, with his wife and daughter.

When he stepped into the car, both women were in their bunks asleep. It was just as well, he thought as he readied himself for bed. He decided he would keep the conversation with young Joshua to himself for now.

THE NEXT DAY, Rachel remained in the car, taking her meals with her mother there. She didn't wish to run into Joshua Thomas again if she could help it. She spent her time reading and looking out the window, watching the scenery pass by as the train progressed down the tracks, taking her farther and farther away from the only home she had ever known.

Her father had been out of the car most of the day, probably visiting with the men he'd met on the train, playing cards or smoking and drinking. He was certainly enjoying the train ride.

But the man had worked in an office all his adult life. She was sure he was relieved to have the free time to indulge in such things.

Her mother was working on the gift for Sarah. So, Rachel was left to her own thoughts. She put down the book she had been reading, leaned her head back and closed her eyes.

She thought of all the parties back home, her friends, the young men who were always trying to get her attention. She doubted there would be such frivolous parties and teas where she was going. What did people do in Oklahoma, she wondered. She had never bothered to ask Sarah.

And now that Joshua would be working for her new brother-in-law, did that mean she would have to see him on a regular basis? She was still trying to process in her mind why on earth the man would wish to go back to Oklahoma once he had been back east and could have stayed there. He must be made of the same cloth as her sister, a bit touched in the head if you asked her.

How anyone, male or female, could choose the wild west over the excitement of the city was beyond her understanding. And Conrad was just as bad! She had been told that he had sold the family business, home, and everything else to join his sister and her family in Oklahoma. Just like her parents were forcing her to do! She still didn't understand why they couldn't have just gone for an extended visit. Why sell everything and relocate there, for goodness' sake?

Aunt Mary, her father's sister, had been more than willing to let her stay with her, but, no, her father had put his foot down on that. His sister had been widowed young, had no children, and was a bit of a social butterfly. Rachel and she would have gotten on famously, she was sure.

Well, soon, she would be with her beloved aunt again.

They were almost halfway to their destination now. In a few more days, they would be stopping for an overnight break, then the next stop would be Oklahoma. Hopefully, the hotel in the town where they stopped for the night would be nice and there would be some decent shops for her to browse. When they finally got to Sarah, the plan was to find a house in town, near Sarah and Conrad. At least her parents weren't going to live on a ranch. For that, she could be grateful. She shuddered at the mere thought.

Finally, it was time to stop. She was anxious to see the town and get out of the train car. Her mother kept her close to her, of course, while their father got rooms for them at the hotel. Rachel couldn't wait to indulge in a proper bath before going to the shops and having dinner.

When she sank down into the warm water, she smiled. Now, this was more like it. The room she had been appointed would pass, she supposed. It was pleasant enough, with a handmade quilt on the bed, frilly curtains at the window, and a table and chair where she could sit with a cup of tea and look out over the bustling town.

Feeling refreshed after the bath and tea, she dressed and went next door to see if her mother was ready to do some shopping.

When she stepped into the hallway, Joshua was coming out of his room across the hall. Wonderful. She tried to ignore him, but he made that impossible.

"Going out to see what the town has to offer?" he asked.

"My mother and I are going shopping before dinner," she said as she knocked on her parents' door.

"Have a nice time," he said as he sauntered down the hall, whistling as he went.

"Ugh," she said as she waited for her mother.

"Ready, dear?" Rosella asked as she opened the door. "We haven't much time, so we should get going." She turned to tell her husband, "We will meet you in the dining room."

"I thought we would go to the dress shop first," Rachel said.

"Fine, Rachel, but we cannot purchase much. We don't have room on the train."

"Yes, Mother, I am aware of that. I just want to look. I don't know what sort of dresses I will be expected to wear out in the uncivilized world."

"You exaggerate so much, dear."

Once inside the shop, she began to look through rack after rack of dresses. Some were fancier than she had imagined they would be, others plainer. Her mother suggested they each buy one of the plainer ones for everyday wear.

She resigned herself to the fact that she probably wasn't going to be able to talk her mother into anything else and chose a pale rose-colored dress with simple ivory lace trim. It was pretty enough but certainly not something she would have been seen in back home.

When they returned to the hotel, her mother had the packages sent up to their rooms and they walked to the dining room where they found her father deep in conversation over coffee with, of all people, Joshua Thomas.

"Well, here are my girls now. Did you buy out the stores?" her father asked as both he and Joshua stood.

"We each bought one dress," her mother replied. "Your bank account is safe."

They sat down and the waitress brought menus and tea for the women.

"I took the liberty of telling her you ladies would have tea when you arrived," Joshua told them with a grin.

Rachel stopped mid-sip, her blue eyes blazing as she said, "And what made you think we would want you to take it upon yourself to do that?"

Her mother gasped, but when she glanced at her father expecting a reprimand for her rudeness, she saw that he was grinning too.

"I didn't, but I thought that after shopping, the two of you would appreciate it," Joshua said calmly as he picked up the menu, ignoring her sigh of disgust. "Now, what looks good on the menu tonight?"

"I suppose you wish to order my food too?" Rachel spat at him, venom in her voice.

"I wasn't thinking that, but since you've said it, yes, I believe I will." He turned to her with a gaze as icy as hers, and then it wasn't. His green eyes darkened with something she couldn't define.

CHAPTER 2

AMY

*H*is handsome face, strong physique, and domineering personality were beginning to infuriate her. The initial excitement and infatuation waned. They married over a week ago and had yet to spend the night together as husband and wife.

"Are you listening to me, Amy?" Glen demanded.

Raised to behave as a lady and to always respect and obey her parents and her husband once she married, it became increasingly difficult for Amy. At least in relation to the latter. She missed her ma. She wished she had her pa to offer strength and guidance. Lord knew she needed it.

Glen's extreme evasiveness no longer intrigued her. It angered her. It troubled her. When the knocking on the door came before sunup and Ruth announced the early caller as Glen, Amy's heart skipped a beat and soared. Had he finally come for her? Did he acquire a place for them to call home?

From his lack of information, she decided not. And having

just woken, the urge to relieve herself made it impossible to listen to his petty commands and his ambiguous reasoning. And completely uncharacteristic of her, she told him such. "No, I am not listening. You show up here at this ridiculous hour and inform me to pack my bag as you won't have me stay with Ruth any longer. You state you and I will not be residing together, but you made other arrangements for me. Why? I'm happy here with Ruth until the day... if it ever comes that we might live together as the married couple that we are."

Stepping up to her, forcing her to step back and into the room, Glen quietly shut the door, closing them inside, and took her hands in his. "I know, angel. I had to come early because I need to get to the drill site. Once I finish my tasks, I'm returning to you. We can take a long walk. Have pie and coffee together. And then I'll escort you to your new residence."

The warmth of his hands, the pleading in his tone, affected her. Her body responded. A rampaging flush heated her from her center outwardly. Her knees weakened and she yearned for him to tug her tightly to him and kiss her until it soothed the unfamiliar aches she suffered in his presence.

But he didn't. He remained where he stood. Once again, he gazed at her. His bright, captivating blue eyes bored into hers—into her—hoping for her approval. "Of course. I will have my bag ready."

A few hours later after he'd rushed away after issuing his directives, and she served the patrons in the hotel restaurant, Amy regretted agreeing to Glen's dictates. He told her she could no longer work there. Supposedly, he had an opportunity for her which would earn them more than double her current weekly pay.

She didn't want to leave her friends. Since his appearance months late, little by little, he isolated her from the people who extended kindness and supported her when she had no one. Most perplexing, he forbade her from having any association with anyone related to the Big G. And he worked there, with a Garrison and others of their kin.

The women of the Big G usually came to town on Saturdays. She watched them out the window while she worked. They were all so pretty. They all appeared so happy. She wished to socialize with them. She envied them.

Amy might have been upset with Lizzie, but she never thought to sever all contact. Glen insisted, and warned if he ever caught her socializing with Lizzie, he would put her over his knees and blister her bottom.

As if. She had never been spanked a day in her life. She never deserved one. Meek and mild. Pretty and boring. Exactly as a true young lady should be.

The activities she wished to indulge in with Glen were anything but. And she couldn't focus on anything else. She couldn't sleep. She had no appetite. Should she be ashamed? Probably. She debated with her conscience, but her bodily instincts won every argument. For goodness' sake, they were married.

Lost in her moral deliberations and her improper dreaming of Glen, it shocked her when arms wrapped around her waist and her back contacted a solid torso. "I have no idea what you are so deep in thought over, but the look on your face sets my blood on fire." Glen breathed into the back of her neck.

She swatted a towel around her and at him. Circling, she surveyed the room and lowered her eyes. "You startled me. You shouldn't greet me... so, so familiarly, in public."

Glen's head fell back, and he laughed. A raucous and gaudy display of amusement. It embarrassed her. She gripped the towel in both hands, wringing it. "Can I get you a slice of pie and some coffee? I must finish my tables. I didn't expect you this soon."

Sadly, she worried if she should expect him at all. Then she dreaded if he did. Leaving Ruth and the restaurant saddened her. Worse—what did he have planned?

"I hoped to be here earlier. As it is, we need be on our way," he stated.

"You said we could take a walk. Have pie together. Though I can't, at the moment. But you can," she countered.

Grazing his fingertips across her forehead, he leaned toward her. "I am disappointed too. I told you I hoped to be here earlier. Conrad called a meeting at the site. I must return." Gripping her hip with his other hand, he slid it lower and patted her bottom. "Now be a good girl. Hurry up and let's be on our way."

The smallest amount of affection he showed her had her racing to do his bidding. Perhaps if she quickened and hastily joined him, they could share a kiss... a little conversation. Anything.

Breathless and sweaty from racing to join him, she found him sitting in the hotel lobby. "All done. I haven't given my farewells to Ruth and my employer, but I can do that later after you return to work," she said.

He stood and grinned. "Perhaps. Show me to your bag."

Perhaps. If she wanted to come and give her friends a proper farewell—she would.

Lifting her bag as if it weighed nothing, Glen toted it through the hotel and outside. Amy glanced around and didn't locate a wagon. He walked away and past several businesses. It initially bothered her thinking she might be staying outside of town, because she had no horse. A false sense of relief came over her. Sure, staying in town since she had no horse seemed logical. But if he intended for her to remain in town, why have her quit her job?

She followed along. He might have a surprise for her. Her stomach fluttered and her heart sang. A home. A night holding each other.

The fantasies she conjured were obliterated.

Huffing from the decent stroll, the heat, and her immature musings, Amy eyed their destination. The establishment, well-kept, and upscale on the outside did not camouflage the disgrace existing beyond the door. "What are we doing here? Are you teasing me?" she sneered.

Dropping her bag on the ground, a poof of dirt rising around it, Glen scoffed, "You are as much a hypocrite as the rest of 'me. What exactly do you think occurs here? I assume you have no idea. We are wed. You won't be giving yourself to another. Ever. But… there are opportunities. Especially for a beautiful woman with your ample assets. Now, replace your scowl with your lovely smile."

As often since she reached age thirteen, men's eyes, Glen's eyes went straight to her bosom when he mentioned assets. She hated her breasts. Too often a man's focus fixated on them. So much so they spoke gibberish and behaved as imbeciles. "I can't go in there. You can't expect me to."

Grasping her shoulders, he lowered his face to hers. "You are young and gorgeous. Our mutual goal is to be together. Is it not? For two people lacking financial means, we are forced to deviate from the conventional course. And you will thank me one day."

She shrugged and stepped away from him. "I don't think so. How could I? I won't. You specify I can no longer keep company with… basically everyone I have come to call a friend. Yet, you recommend I not only inhabit but profit at a brothel?"

"It is not a brothel, Amy. Give it a chance. You are imagining the saloon girls. This is a discreet upscale establishment. Select men, if not frequent patrons, must be invited in by Lola. And they pay upon entry," Glen explained.

She didn't care how he hoped to vindicate it. "If it is so discreet, how come I know of it and its activities?" she implored.

His lips parted and she watched his tongue curl around his upper teeth and scrub across them. Dropping his eyes to the ground, he sighed. "Because it handles its affairs inconspicuously in comparison to a saloon, people are ignorant to the truth. This is between you and me. No one need know. I swear to you, Lola and the other ladies won't entertain gossip."

"I don't understand how this can aid us—in any form. I refuse," she declared.

The man she envisioned as tender and nice, transformed. He accused, "You are badgering me and what would your father think of you behaving this way? You are being immature and unaccommodating. This isn't home. This is a new territory. Stop judging and start reciprocating. I can't do it alone."

Her head spun. Nothing resonated positive in any manner. He brought her there. He promised a simple life. This was anything but simple. And she felt manipulated. She should return home. The very mention of her father gave her pause. He would never agree to what Glen suggested. Never.

"Please get me home. I will pay the fare. I have a little money from working at the restaurant," she stated. Nothing about anything seemed appropriate. Lizzie tried to alert her to not rush into anything with Glen. Amy recognized it before then, but she detested admitting failure.

Glen picked up her bag. "Let us go and procure you a return ticket. I realize this hasn't proven to be what you dreamed of. But it could. Don't you believe the things worth having are sometimes the things we least expect? The very ones that push us beyond ourselves?"

Her anger surged. "You sent for me. How can you promise me one thing and deliver nothing? Except a life of me compromising my morals?"

He ushered her inside. The red draperies and the scantily clad women she glimpsed sounded bells in her head. Darting from the foyer, Glen caught her wrist. "Stop. I will turn you over my knee." Yanking her into his side, he lowered his mouth to her ear and whispered, "It does involve baring what some claim is an unacceptable amount of skin. It's dancing and singing dressed in a visible corset. A shorter skirt. Bare shoulders. All you do is persuade gentlemen to buy drinks. Dance with them. Sing to them. They pay for your time and attention."

"I will never be accepted by the women I wish to befriend. Never," she whined.

"You never will anyway. Because I already forbade it," he reminded.

"And who do we have here?" interrupted a flamboyant, older, attractive woman. She wore a brightly colored ruffled skirt which only reached her knees. A visible red petticoat barely reached her boots. Her lips were painted the same color. "You must be Amy. I'm Lola. I have heard so much about you and am excited to have you." Positioning her hands on her hips, she seductively posed and winked at Glen. "She is just as you described... lovely. A perfect addition."

Glen removed his hat and dipped his head at Lola. "I wouldn't dare deceive you, Miss Lola."

One of her eyebrows lifted as she attested, "I thought not. Those who have tried regret it." Raising her bare arm in the air, she snapped her fingers. "Josie, take Amy upstairs. Show her to her room and dress her for the evening."

A skinny redhead with lips to match approached. Amy looked to Glen. She willed him to speak up and bring a halt to his ridiculous and insulting notion. He did not. He stepped away from her and averted his gaze.

"Don't worry about your bag. Virgil will bring it up. You won't be needing it until evening's end," Josie stated. The woman couldn't be much older than Amy. She had kind eyes and a sweet smile.

Following Josie to the stairs, Amy viewed a large parlor room on the left. She observed several other women laughing with gentlemen. The room was large and contained several sofas and chairs and a piano on the far end. It smelled of cigars. She found a dining area to the right. Both rooms were lavishly decorated. Beautiful. Amy had never stayed anywhere as luxurious.

Upstairs, they entered a long hallway. Josie took her to the fourth door on the right. Again, the furnishings and decorations surprised and thrilled her.

"This is your room. Behind the screen are a few garments Lola provided until you can purchase your own. On the dresser you have perfume and lip stain. Lola insists we use it. She is usually easy-going, but if you cross her... not so much." Josie sat in a beautifully upholstered chair. "Go on and get dressed. We have a full house this evening."

Amy's heart pounded in her chest. "Is Glen still here?"

Josie smirked. "He's still here, darlin'. He's one who enjoys a cigar and a few bourbons."

How had it not entered her mind before? Glen frequented the establishment. He kept company with these women.

AFTER THE FIRST NIGHT, it came easy and satisfying, working and living at Lola's. The men she spent time with were content with conversation and her singing. She had always had a great singing voice and having the opportunity to use it for such an appreciative audience and receive payment pleased her beyond her wildest dreams.

Some of the women did entertain patrons upstairs, but no one ever requested she do so. She even had regular customers. Mr. O'Brien, a sweet, elderly widower visited on Tuesday evenings. He shared a fine meal with her in the dining room before moving to the parlor and having her sing while he played the piano. He surprised her with gifts or flowers each visit.

Mr. Ramsey came on Thursday. He had lost an eye and several fingers in an accident. A quiet man. He urged her to tell him about her life back east. He, too, often brought gifts and he enjoyed reading poetry to her.

Glen came on Saturday. He stayed for a cigar and bourbon

and took her week's pay before he left. Odd, she didn't think of him often any longer. It didn't seem as if he gave her much thought, either. He never suggested they spend time together outside of Lola's. He never initiated she sit with him and share anything together. And she took Josie's advice and didn't hand over all her earnings each week. Why should she? She might have need for it herself.

"Did Glen ever come upstairs?" she inquired to Josie one afternoon as they prepared to go shopping.

Josie shook her head and narrowed her eyes. "Your husband is not a topic I wish to discuss with you," she remarked.

"Isn't it abnormal for a man not to share a bed with his wife? I wonder if he is unable. Physically." Amy never witnessed him showing attention to any of the other girls. But it didn't necessarily mean he had not in the past. "Perhaps he finds me unappealing."

Chuckling, Josie insisted, "No man, whether capable or not, could find you unappealing."

"I can't make sense of it. I've tried to give him the benefit of the doubt, but it's getting harder and harder to do so."

Repositioning Amy's hat, Josie smiled and cupped her face. "You must speak to him. From what you told me when you first arrived, he has a goal. Maybe, he wishes to postpone until he can move out of the bunkhouse at the ranch and provide you a fine home."

"Yes. You are right. I am being impatient. "Taking a deep breath, Amy returned Josie's smile. "Let's be on our way."

The townspeople paid little attention to them when they ventured outside of the house and strolled and shopped. They had money. They dressed in eye-catching finery. Amy never believed she would ever own such garments.

Making her purchases, Amy told Josie she would wait outside. A steady breeze blew, making the summer day not as oppressive as it would be without it. Locating a bench, she took a seat and watched the people go about their day. In the alleyway behind her, she heard a woman sobbing.

Her instincts urged her to extend a friendly hand—offer any assistance and convey her concern. But the woman hid in the alley. Did she wish to be left alone? Amy sat and attempted to ignore it and not intrude, but the crying continued.

Hesitantly, she stood and rounded the corner. She surveyed the area but didn't see anyone. Hearing sniffling, she continued along the narrow path and found a woman crouched between stacked crates. "Are you all right?" she asked.

The woman didn't lift her head. Holding her hands in front of her face, she nodded. Amy couldn't walk away. The woman needed a friend.

"Are you injured? If you aren't harmed, what can be so terrible?" she pressed.

The woman dropped her hands. *Lizzie.* Lizzie stared at her with tear-soaked eyes. "Amy? Is that you?" she questioned.

Well, she supposed she didn't look like Lizzie remembered her. Reaching out, she offered Lizzie her hand. "Come on. Stand. Tell me what has you so distraught."

Wobbling, Lizzie took her hand and started sobbing again. "Where have you been? Why are you dressed... as you are? Has Glen gone and left you to manage on your own?" She retrieved a handkerchief from her purse and wiped her eyes and blew her nose.

"Oh no. Glen is still at the Big G. All is well with me. But what about you?"

Taking a shaky, rattling, deep breath, Lizzie fretted, "I will figure it out. I have worried about you. I pray you are no longer angry with me."

"I was never angry with you. And honestly, I regret discounting your advice. Not that I regret my marriage. Now, please tell me what you has so upset."

Shooting her eyes to the sky as they once again filled with

tears, Lizzie pleaded, "I can't. I can't tell anyone. No one can ever know."

Her friend's pain hurt her. She worried she would cry. "Lizzie, please. You can tell me anything. I would never betray your confidence. Never. I too have things I prefer stay between you and me."

"I'm pregnant, "Lizzie blurted. Her knees buckled and she sobbed on the ground.

Why this made Lizzie unhappy, Amy couldn't comprehend. "You and Floyd don't want to start a family."

"It… it's not his child," Lizzie wailed.

Not what Amy expected. Lizzie had been unfaithful. "Have you told the father? Do you love him? Would you choose him?"

"No… no, no. It's Slater's. He forced himself on me," Lizzie confessed.

It took a moment for the name 'Slater' to register. When it did, Amy empathized with her friend. Slater had caused quite a ruckus before his arrest and subsequent murder. And she realized Lizzie said he raped her. Amy felt sick. Biting her lip between her front teeth, she sat on the ground in front of Lizzie and took her hands in hers. "You aren't alone. You have me. Together we will find a solution. I promise."

CHAPTER 3

RACHEL

*R*achel's first look at her new town was limited. It was raining, and she hurried to the platform with her mother to find a dry spot as her father took care of their luggage.

Sarah and Conrad would be here somewhere to greet them, but with the crowd and the rain, they hadn't spotted them yet. Not that she knew what her brother-in-law looked like. Would she recognize her sister? Had she changed?

Then she spotted them. *Joshua* was talking to a young, attractive couple, and when the woman turned, Rachel gasped. It was Sarah, and she was positively glowing with happiness. Then, horror of horrors, Joshua led them to her and her mother.

"Here they are," he said as he stood back with Conrad to allow Sarah to hug her mother and sister.

"Mama!" Sarah's arms were around their mother and when she finally let her go, she turned to Rachel. "Sissy, you're all grown up."

"You haven't been gone that long," Rachel reminded her.

Mr. Linton joined them, having sent their bags on to the hotel. He pulled Sarah to him. "Sweetheart, it's so good to see you."

"Oh, Papa, I'm so happy you are here. Let me introduce you to Conrad." She took her husband's hand. "Mama, Papa, Rachel, this is my husband, Conrad Appleby."

Mr. Linton shook the man's hand. "It's a pleasure to meet you, Conrad."

Then Conrad took her mother's hand and said, "I'm happy to finally meet you, ma'am."

Rachel was sizing him up. Not bad looking, her sister could have done worse. He took her hand and said, "Ah, the lovely Rachel. I've heard so much about you from Sarah. She is so happy to have you here."

"Thank you," she responded.

Mr. Linton spoke up. "We met Joshua on the train. He tells us he will be working for you."

"Yes, I stole him away from my brother-in-law on the ranch," Conrad said with a chuckle. He looked at Joshua and said, "How was the trip back home? Everything go all right?"

"As well as could be expected," was all Joshua said.

"Well, how about we all go to the restaurant for lunch?" Conrad suggested. "I'm sure you are all famished and ready to settle in."

"I have the guest room ready," Sarah said.

"Oh, thank you, dear, but we have arranged for rooms at the hotel. You are a newlywed, and we don't wish to impose. We will begin looking for a house right away," her mother said.

"I have been looking into that for you. I'll tell you about a few houses that are available while we have lunch," Conrad said.

"Oh, that sounds wonderful," Rosella said. "Doesn't it, George?" she asked as she turned to her husband.

"Indeed, it does. Hopefully, we'll be able to look at them soon," he agreed.

When they reached the hotel, George went to the desk to check them in while the others waited for him before going into the restaurant for lunch.

Rachel looked around. It was a nice enough establishment, she guessed. She spotted a young couple walking through the lobby from the restaurant. The man seemed to be in a hurry. The woman wasn't looking any too pleased but she hurried along to keep up with him.

"Come on, Amy," the man said.

Just then her father joined them, saying the staff would take their bags to their rooms. They all went into the restaurant for lunch.

Once they'd ordered, Rachel tried to relax and enjoy her tea. She listened to her mother and sister for a while, then turned her attention to the men. Conrad was telling her father about the houses he'd found that were for sale, and Joshua was listening.

"I think the one on Rosedale sounds promising. A two-story, with three bedrooms and a water closet," her father was saying.

"I'll speak to the owner when we leave here about showing it to you," Conrad said pleasantly.

Rachel's attention was drawn back to the women when Sarah asked if she would accompany her and their mother to the ladies' powder room.

"THE SOONER WE can get settled, the better. We are hoping this new environment will be good for Rachel," Mr. Linton commented to Conrad when he saw his daughters leave the table.

"Some problems there?" Conrad asked.

Joshua grinned but said nothing.

"Not yet, but I fear it was brewing. My sister, even though I love her dearly, is not the best influence on her. Mary married at a young age, to an older, wealthy man. It wasn't a love match, and when he passed, she was left a very wealthy young widow. Instead of settling down again, I'm afraid my sister chose to be the belle of the ball, so to speak. She enjoys the company of several men, rather than just one. I can understand that she may be gun shy about marrying again, after the disastrous first marriage that was more or less arranged by our parents, God rest their souls. However, it was obvious that Rachel was growing fond of the same kind of life, so it was time to get her away from the city. We miss Sarah, so it made sense to come here. I only hope it is a good move for Rachel. She was very upset when we refused to allow her to stay in Philadelphia with Mary, even though Mary would have gladly let her," Mr. Linton confided in a low tone, so others wouldn't hear.

"I see," Conrad said. "I think you've made a wise choice in coming here. Isn't that right, Joshua?"

"Oh, yes, I heartily agree. And having met Miss Rachel on the train, I can tell you that her parents' concern is warranted. She just needs the right man to set her straight."

Conrad chuckled. "And might you be that man?"

"We shall see, now won't we?" he returned with a grin.

"Sounds like things may get interesting around here, eh?" Conrad looked at his father-in-law and winked.

"I can assure you, with Rachel, it's bound to," George replied with a wry laugh.

The ladies returned to the table, so the men shifted the conversation to Conrad's business. Their meal arrived soon after and they enjoyed the delicious food. Then when lunch was over, Joshua excused himself to head to the ranch, where he currently lived in the bunkhouse. Even though he now worked for

Conrad, the Garrisons allowed him to remain at the ranch since he would be working on the rig there.

"I will see you bright and early tomorrow morning at the rig. Tonight, I'm going to get some shut eye," he said to Conrad after he'd told the others goodbye.

Conrad went to see the owners of the house on Rosedale while his in-laws settled in at the hotel. Sarah remained behind to help her family unpack and visit a while longer.

When Conrad returned, he told them they had an appointment the next morning at ten to view the home. After that, he and Sarah invited the Lintons to their house to see their home and to enjoy a light supper.

"Oh, I'm anxious to see the house," Rosella said. "I think it's lovely the way you and Johnny's sister traded homes."

"Yes, it worked out well. The house is small. Someday, we will either have to enlarge it or look for something bigger, but for now it suits us fine. I want to take you out to meet Kate and Jim and see the ranch one day soon, too," Sarah said enthusiastically.

"We'll look forward to that. I also would like to see Conrad's operation if he wouldn't mind," George said.

"I wouldn't mind at all. I would be happy to show you around and get your opinion on some things, sir," Conrad answered.

"And of course, we can introduce you to many of our friends at church on Sunday," Sarah said.

Rachel was quiet as they rode in Conrad's wagon to her sister's house. She glanced around at the shops and looked at the people milling around, doing their daily business. She wondered about their lives.

When they pulled up in front of a quaint, yellow painted house, with white shutters and a front porch with a swing, she thought it was cute but small. Not exactly what her sister was used to.

The men helped the ladies out and they all went inside. Sarah proudly gave them a tour of the two-bedroom home. She showed them the bedrooms, then Conrad's little home office, before moving on to the dining room, living room and kitchen. There was a water closet and a place for Sarah to wash clothes on the back porch. She had a line strung up in the back yard to hang them to dry. There was a small shed in the back that Conrad told them was for the horse and wagon.

"It's a wonderful home for a newlywed couple," Rosella exclaimed.

"Yes, very nice," her husband agreed.

"Rachel, what do you think? Think you'd like to visit every once in a while and stay in our guest room? It would be like old times," Sarah asked her sister.

"Perhaps, although I doubt your husband wants guests so soon after the wedding," Rachel said, looking over at Conrad.

"It would be nice for Sarah to have the company when I have to go to Oklahoma City for business," he replied.

THEY SAT and chatted over tea and coffee and then Mrs. Linton helped Sarah get supper on the table. Conrad talked with Rachel in an attempt to get to know this feisty little sister of his wife's. He was curious to know if Joshua was right about her.

By the time supper was served, he was convinced that the girl needed a good hard spanking on her backside. She was snobbish and spoiled as far as he could tell. Joshua just might be right. If the boy thought he was man enough to tame this wild child, more power to him. Rachel might be beautiful, but her disposition would turn the men in this area away rather quickly. He doubted they would need to worry, however, since the girl had made it plain she felt she was above ranchers and cowboys. He wondered what she thought about roughnecks, and he laughed to himself.

Joshua sure had his work cut out for him. Conrad didn't envy him at all.

~

THE NEXT DAY, Sarah accompanied her parents and sister to see the house on Rosedale. Conrad was working but he told them he would be at the office if they needed anything.

The owners were an elderly couple. They told the Lintons that they were moving in with their daughter and her family on their ranch, as the house was too much for them to take care of these days.

The home was beautifully decorated and Mr. and Mrs. Brown told them they would leave any of the furnishings they wanted except for a few things they wished to keep.

"That works out perfectly since we left behind most of our furniture. We planned to buy more once we found a home, but it looks like we may not need to," Rosella said as she looked around. They went up the stairs to look at the bedrooms. Downstairs, there was a living room, dining room, nice-sized kitchen and mud room. Of course, there was a water closet. A wraparound porch completed the tour. Out back, was a building to keep a horse and wagon or carriage. There was one other small room that could be used as a library or office off the entry. There was a stairway near the entrance but also one in the kitchen.

Sarah asked Rachel her opinion, but the girl just shrugged. It wasn't like she was going to be here long anyway. "It's fine," she said. "I like the window seat in the one bedroom. Perhaps that could be my room." She looked at her mother.

"Of course, dear. I was thinking the same thing." Rosella looked at George. "What do you think?"

"I believe I wish to sit down with Mr. Brown and do some talking."

Mrs. Brown spoke up. "While the men are hashing things out, why don't we go into the kitchen and I'll make us some tea. I baked cookies yesterday. We'll have some of those if it won't spoil your lunch."

"Oh, cookies and tea would be lovely," Sarah said. "We'll just have a later lunch."

Rosella agreed, and Rachel followed them into the kitchen. She would have much preferred to stay at the hotel or visit the shops, but she knew not to ask. Her father would have immediately refused the request, insisting she accompany them. So, rather than having to hear him say no, she had tagged along like a good daughter. She couldn't wait until she could start causing real trouble around here.

Her thoughts drifted to Joshua. He must be hard at work, doing whatever it was he did. How anyone in his right mind could give up a comfortable life, a good job in the family business, to do the dirty work he would have paid men back home to do, was still a mystery to her. Of course, she didn't know that his job was dirty, but drilling for oil, working on a rig, sounded like dirty work to her. She shuddered, thinking how he must look after a hard day on the job.

Her thoughts were interrupted when Mrs. Brown placed a plate of cookies and a cup of tea in front of her. "And how do you like our little town so far, Miss Linton? Quite a bit different from the city, eh?"

"Oh, well, I-I haven't seen too much of it yet. The hotel is nice enough. The restaurant there had good food yesterday. I would like to browse in some of the shops when I have the time," she said politely. After all, she was a lady and she had been taught to be respectful of her elders.

"There will be plenty of time for shopping once we get settled, Rachel dear," her mother said. "I will need some things for the house."

Just then, the men joined them.

"Well, Ma, can you be packed up within two weeks?" Mr. Brown asked.

"Why, surely, I can. You know Annie and the kids will help, as well as Henry and some of his ranch hands. And I imagine we are leaving some things for these nice folks?"

"We're going to let you women decide on that," George said.

"Let me get you men some coffee and cookies, and then Mrs. Linton and I can walk around again so she can decide what she wishes us to leave."

"Rachel, while they are doing that, why don't you and I walk over to Conrad's office? We can take lunch to him," Sarah suggested.

"All right," Rachel agreed. Anything to get her out of helping her mother choose furniture.

They walked back to Sarah's house and she fixed a basket lunch for her husband, with sandwiches and fruit. She put a thermos of lemonade in as well.

"Do you take him lunch every day?" Rachel asked.

"Not every day. Sometimes he comes home, but there are many days when he is out working and not in the office, so we like to have lunch together when we can."

"Hmm," was all Rachel said in response.

"Oh, someday, you'll be fixing lunch for your husband, too, "Sarah teased.

"Not likely," Rachel said under her breath. But she smiled at her sister when she was ready to go, and they walked the short distance to Conrad's office, which was located upstairs in the building the bank was in. There were a few other offices there as well.

"This is his office? I guess I expected something bigger," Rachel said when they walked up the stairs and entered the hallway.

"Well, his business is just starting. Hopefully, someday, he will have his own office building," Sarah said proudly.

They walked in the door that said *Appleby Oil* on the front and a young woman sat at a desk.

"Hello, Gertie. Is Conrad around?" Sarah asked.

"Yes, go on in. He and Mr. Thomas are going over a few things. I see you've brought him lunch. How sweet."

"Gertie's husband works for Conrad, out at the drilling site," Sarah explained to Rachel as they entered the door that led into Conrad's office.

"What is Joshua doing here? Doesn't he work at the site too?" Rachel asked, confused.

Sarah smiled. "Yes, I imagine Conrad is familiarizing Joshua with some things. It's his first day, you know."

"Oh, yes, that's right. I forgot."

Conrad looked up and smiled in greeting. "Hello, ladies. How did house hunting go?"

"Papa and Mr. Brown struck a deal. They are even leaving some of the furnishings, and I believe I heard Mr. Brown say they would be out in two weeks," Sarah told him.

"Goodness, that was fast. I'm happy they liked the house," Conrad said.

"And what about you, Miss Linton. Did you like it?" Joshua asked.

"It was fine. I chose the bedroom with the window seat. It reminded me of my room back home."

"I've brought lunch. There is enough for both of you," Sarah said.

"You ladies are joining us, aren't you?" Conrad asked.

"Not today. I want to take Rachel around to some of the shops and introduce her to some folks in town. She can meet the others at church on Sunday."

"Thank you for the lunch, ma'am," Joshua said.

"You are quite welcome. Make sure my husband lets you take a break to enjoy it. Work will still be there after you've eaten."

Conrad chuckled, and Joshua grinned.

"I'll see you at home later. I'm sure Mama and Papa will be busy this afternoon and evening making plans for their new home and arranging for their things to be shipped. Rachel, come along."

"Goodbye, Miss Linton, Mrs. Appleby," Joshua said.

"Have a good afternoon. I should be home around five," Conrad said.

After they left the office, Sarah said, "Joshua seems like a nice young man."

"Do not. Just do not," Rachel said.

"Do not what? I was just making a statement," Sarah said with a side glance at her sister. Was that a slight blush staining her cheeks?

They went to the dress shop first. Rachel looked at some of the creations and was told someone named Annabelle had made them.

"Annabelle is a friend of mine. She was on the same train as Conrad and me on the way out here. You will meet her Sunday. She does wonderful work. In fact, she made both of my wedding dresses," Sarah said. "She is married to Clyde Gonzalez. He also works for Conrad."

Next, they went to the general store, where Rachel looked around. She chose some specialty teas and some candy before they left. Sarah purchased a few food items, and then they walked back to Sarah's house to drop them off before Sarah walked her back to the hotel.

"Will you be all right to walk home alone?" Rachel asked.

"Oh, heavens, of course. This isn't Philadelphia," Sarah told her.

Well, what a good bit of information to know, Rachel thought. *If that is true, it may be easier for me to slip away by myself when the time comes for me to return home to Aunt Mary.* She stored that away in her mind for a later date.

Alone in her room after dinner that evening, her thoughts

drifted to Joshua. He had looked quite handsome today in Conrad's office. He had been wearing denims and a plain shirt. He had boots on his feet, and she had seen a cowboy hat on the desk. Even though cowboys and roughnecks weren't her cup of tea, it didn't mean she couldn't look.

CHAPTER 4

AMY

*W*ho had she become? Someone she didn't know or trust to make sound, sensible decisions. She told Lizzie—poor, hopeless Lizzie—she would help her. She actually said, *'You aren't alone. You have me. Together we will find a solution. I promise.'*

And why? Why would she do that? Glen demanded she not keep company with Lizzie or anyone related to the Big G in any way. And not only did she disregard his command, but she involved herself in a precarious and immoral situation.

Bouncing back and forth between her duty to her husband, her devotion to a friend, and the values instilled in her by her loving, righteous parents—tested her to the point of exhaustion. "Josie, I am not feeling well. I am going to my room to rest for a bit," she informed the one friend at the Parlor she trusted. Yes, she trusted Josie. And Josie had insight and knowledge she didn't, and in order to keep her promise to Lizzie, she required it. Clutching the slender woman's wrist, Amy tugged her along.

Leaning into her ear, she whispered, "I have a favor to ask. I don't know why I didn't think of it before."

And she didn't. Because Glen deposited her at the Parlor and she assumed the duties expected at such an establishment, well, at least a questionable amount of them, her mind slowed. Most likely because it focused on her blemished soul and reputation. It hadn't been a bad experience. It hadn't been oppressive or degrading. Now, it had a purpose.

Pulling Josie inside her room and closing the door, Amy began, "I am not inquiring on your personal use, or prying, but you must have knowledge of an elixir women use when... when," she stalled. How could she say it aloud? It made it a reality. She, a respectable, mild-mannered lady, needed to know how to end a pregnancy.

Josie's golden eyes brightened and widened. She gripped Amy's hands and led her to the bed to sit. "You are in that way. You don't want it? Glen has proven his love for you?"

"Huh? No, not me. You believe Glen loves me?" Amy asked.

Stiffening and shuffling off the bed, Josie deflected, "It's not you? He impregnated another woman?"

"No!" Amy stood and confronted Josie. "You inquired as to if Glen proved his love for me. Yet you wonder if he got another woman with child. Explain. Please."

Squinting, a fire building in her amber eyes, Josie stressed, "You mention a favor. You encourage me upstairs. You... you," she stuttered and leaned in, lowering her voice. "Someone, I suppose, requires assistance in alleviating themselves of an unwanted child. It's not you. I am curious as to any child you would choose to aid in eliminating."

"I won't betray a confidence. I am sorry if I assumed incorrectly, but I did assume you have knowledge of women in similar predicaments over the years," Amy explained.

Crossing her arms under her chest, the motion and the coyly, suggestive gesture lifting her small breasts higher and prominently, Josie purred, "I have attained wealth in many forms over my time as a 'working' gal. I can't be seen engaging in such a thing. Miss Lola would be outraged. She insists these situations are limited to only her girls and are handled discreetly under her supervision. So, without informing her, we will handle it as such. Tomorrow at noon. Outside of the dress shop. The price varies, so bring your purse."

Unable to resist, Amy threw her arms around the thin woman and hugged and rocked her. "Thank you. From the bottom of my heart. You are truly a best friend. Something I've never had."

Josie sighed and broke out of her embrace. She raised her hands palms up framing Amy's face. "Hey, don't thank me yet. It's not always successful. If it's not, the next alternative is worse. But one step at a time."

Throwing her arm around the petite woman again, she hugged her tightly and sighed a breath of relief. She could prevail. Others might condemn her and judge her for currently living a life as a wanton woman, but she knew her truth. She lived a sundry life for sure. But both of her personas pleased her. If she didn't work at the Parlor and have Josie as a friend, she couldn't fathom how she could help Lizzie. That could not be denied.

She busied herself in preparing for the evening and worried over the exchange the next day. It didn't necessarily surprise her when an unexpected caller arrived at sundown and asked for her. After Lizzie confided to her, she only wished to comfort her friend and provided the address of her current residence. Lizzie told her she would send someone for further instructions.

Overhearing Violet speaking to Lola about the uninvited guest asking for her, Amy intervened. "I expected him."

Violet's mouth fell open. She stared at Amy in an unsettling manner before refocusing her attention back to Lola and continuing, "It wasn't I who misled Amy. I can't imagine who did. I believe we all understand we only admit gentlemen. But the caller is one of those Mexicans living on the Big G expansion."

Who did Amy expect? Floyd? She didn't expect anyone. She did. But she didn't. It's not as if Lizzie would have come to the Parlor. Obviously one of Lizzie's relatives came. A male one. Not that she imagined a female would. "I acknowledge he is not our usual client sort, but I assure you he can pay and is safe."

Lola scoffed, "I am disappointed. Your husband vouched for you. We don't allow any non-whites in here. I manage a refined business catering to sophisticated patrons."

The comments rubbed Amy the wrong way. They were prejudicial and untrue. And Amy couldn't idly adhere to them. "I mean no disrespect, Miss Lola, but Mr. Rucker is a cook for the small Purcell farm. Mr. Utley is a blacksmith. This area is home to many of Mexican descent now. Are we to discount them?"

Lifting her chin and eyeing Amy, Lola cautioned, "Valid reasoning. Before he steps through the door, I want the fee. He is not allowed upstairs, and Mr. Jernigan will be informed."

Swallowing past the boulder in her throat, Amy gulped loudly. Informing Glen would bring a mountain of interrogations and reproach on her. It must be. She made a promise. It's not as if anything she had or had not done garnered any attention from her new husband. "I don't entertain my guests upstairs anyway. If you will allow me one minute to relieve myself and reapply my lip color, I shall return."

Racing to the stairs, her shorter skirt provided the ease of taking them two at a time. Ripping out the top drawer of her bureau and reaching behind it, she retrieved her hidden earnings and separated out the entry amount before returning the bundle to its secret spot. She folded and concealed the remaining wad in her hand and returned to the foyer.

It appalled her to discover the front door closed and her guest not awaiting her. Pinning what she hoped were steely eyes on Lola and Violet, she sneered, "You kept him waiting outside? Shame on you."

"Your visit will be conducted in the library," Lola retorted.

As if having a private meeting with him away from prying eyes and ears would bother her. Opening the door, she found a handsome, sweet smiling man. He stretched his hand out. "I am Jose. And you are Amy?"

Nodding, she swung the door wider and returned his smile. Accepting his hand, she acknowledged, "I am Amy. I apologize for the delay. Please come inside." Feeling the money in her palm, his eyes displayed his confusion, but he cautiously entered, and she shut the door behind him. Spinning to Lola, she flipped her hand revealing the fee. Lola yanked it from her, and she and Violet left the entryway.

Advising Jose to follow her, Amy led him down the hall past the dining room and parlor room and to the library. Gesturing him inside, she shut the door and urged him take a seat.

"Amy, I am confused as to why I am here. What type of establishment is this? Why are you here? Lizzie failed to inform me of anything other than calling upon you and bringing her some item you have for her." He cocked his head to the side peering at her. Warm, dark eyes framed with the longest, blackest eyelashes she had ever seen, bored into hers, begging for answers. When she failed to provide any, he reached in his pocket and withdrew some bills. "I don't know how much you paid for my entrance, but I am a proud man and will repay you."

Placing her hand over his, she declined. "It is not my intention to disrespect you, but please... I deeply regret the treatment you received. I consider Lizzie a dear friend and that encompasses any and all who are dear to her." His fingers were rough and hot. Realizing she kept her hand over his far longer than she should have, she jerked it away from his.

The motion obviously jostled her breasts heaving over the top of the unyielding corset as his eyes fixated on them. Embarrassed, she stepped deeper into the room and out of his direct view.

"No need to concern yourself with it. It won't be the first nor the last time me or my kin have been shunned because of our darker coloring. And if payment is expected for the opportunity to socialize with you, I will pay. The opportunities in this area are broader and lucrative, much more than the life I had in Texas. I spoke with Conrad Appleby, and he has offered me a position with his oil company."

"That is incredible news. What an exciting opportunity," she remarked. Would he be working alongside Glen? Lola already stated she would tell Glen of her caller. But would she? And if she didn't, would Jose speak of it? Not that any of it mattered. She made Lizzie a promise. She kept her promises. "The item I'm obtaining for Lizzie won't be available until tomorrow at noon. Can you meet me at Daisy's dress shop then?"

Inwardly, she jumped as his hands grasped her shoulders gently from behind her. She enjoyed his touch. She appreciated his unimposing demeanor. "I will meet you anywhere, anytime, Miss Amy."

She should correct him. No longer a Miss, but a Mrs., but the inclination evaded her. Circling toward him, she insisted, "Sit with me. Your time is paid, and I am enjoying your company."

A huge smile brightened his already glowing persona. "I would like nothing more."

And neither would she.

They sat together laughing and talking for almost two hours. She immediately discovered him to be a quick-witted and jovial gentleman. The conversation he steered toward her and her family, but not once did he inquire into why she resided and worked at the Parlor. He seemed genuinely interested in her—regardless of her current circumstances. He told her that he and Lizzie were cousins, and he elaborated on their family, and it shocked her to hear how many of them actually relocated from

Texas. It sounded as if they had an entire town population living on the property. The tales of the children's antics had her crying in fits of laughter and begging him to give her a minute to catch her breath.

A knock on the door interrupted their fun. The door opened and Violet poked her head inside. "You have another caller, Amy."

Amy acknowledged her, but the woman didn't leave until Amy stood and gave her farewells to Jose. "Thank you for a wonderfully, unexpected evening. Until we meet again," she stated and winked at him, her back to Violet.

Grasping her hand in his, he lifted it to his lips. Smooth, soft lips made contact with the back of her hand. He spoke into it. "And we will." Releasing her hand, he winked back at her and mouthed, "Tomorrow. Noon."

"Lola told me to have you take him through the kitchen to exit," Violet added.

Rolling her eyes and sighing, the mere mention of such boiling her blood. Amy started to voice her disapproval when Jose chuckled and kissed her on the cheek advising, "Be a good girl, Amy. As if you could be anything but."

HER THOUGHTS REMAINED ON JOSE. Throughout her next engagement and dream-filled sleep, he occupied her mind. She woke early and started her chores. She giggled recalling the stories he told. She warmed remembering the touch of his fingers and his lips on her skin.

Finishing her laundry and completing her kitchen tasks, she went upstairs to dress for the noon meeting. After bathing, she devoted an unusual amount of effort to her hair. She chose an outfit, though lurid, a little less than her usual pick. It's not as if Jose didn't know how she provided for herself. Well, provided for Glen. *Glen.* A rush of guilt overcame her. She had become a... a debauched woman. Not by choice. Glen instigated it. He married her. He neglected her. He placed her in an unscrupulous position.

A knock came, intruding on her unhappy musings. Josie glanced at her, looked back over her shoulder, and remarked, "Don't you look extra pretty today. My, oh my. I wonder who has the lovely Amy all stressed with her appearance." Darting her head again into the hallway, she stepped inside. "I'm leaving now. I have what you seek. You have ten minutes. Daisy's shop."

"Yep. Don't worry. I understand," Amy replied.

Until she saw Jose pacing in front of the shop and Josie sauntering up to it, the possible and probable repercussions eluded her. She betrayed Glen. She planned to betray Lola. She accepted a role in terminating a pregnancy. And she yearned to spend time with Jose. Nothing good could come of any of it. As it shouldn't.

Marching across the road to intercept and to mediate any impediment which might arise between Jose and Josie, Jose's broad smile and pleasing acknowledgment stunned her. Her knees weakened. She envisioned them giving out completely and him scooping her up in his arms and into his solid chest. In his embrace, she would have everything she needed and wanted. A man who adored her. A man devoted to her. A man who shared everything and held no secrets.

She had a traitorous heart and an adulterous body. Sprinting to her, Jose offered his arm and escorted her out of the bustle of horses and carts and onto the walkway. "You look stunning today," he commented. An instant rush of heat flooded her neck and face.

Spotting Jose and Amy, Josie appeared flustered. She snatched Amy's arm and pulled her aside. "I believed I stressed to you the criticality of required discretion in this matter. You expect me to conduct this reprehensible exchange in the presence of a Tejano?"

Now Josie referred rudely to Jose and behaved as if he revolted her. A completely opposite heat from the one a moment before spread through her. Amy seethed, "Yes, I do. The recipient and I trust him implicitly. I am unable to deliver to her. Jose will."

"Give me five dollars," snapped Josie. She thrust her hand in between them and positioned herself to hide their transaction. Amy placed the money in her hand, and she withdrew a vial of yellow liquid. "One dose tonight. Two tomorrow. Three the next day. If it's unsuccessful, twenty dollars to meet with the 'female physician' next Tuesday morning at seven."

Josie hurried off before she could thank her. Circling to Jose, she took his hand and placed the vial in his palm. She repeated the instructions given to her by Josie but excluded the part about the physician. She didn't know what all Lizzie had told him.

"Is Lizzie in trouble? Is she ill?" he asked. His brown eyes were dismal with concern.

Her mouth went dry. She hated lying to him. It physically pained her. "No. No, it is for her monthly cramps," she muttered.

He gripped her hand and squeezed it. "May I call on you again? Tonight?" he requested.

Over his shoulder, she glimpsed Glen. His eyes found her, and they narrowed and exposed a fury that had her trembling. Jerking her hand out of Jose's, she replied, "Yes." Bolting into the road, she ran to the hotel. Going into the restaurant, she went into the kitchen and asked Mrs. Wilson if she had any bread pudding she could purchase.

The sweet lady delighted in receiving praise for her cooking and without hesitation packed up a generous serving and declined compensation. "We all miss you so much. I sure wish you would come back. Even if only a day over the weekend. You were one of the best servers I ever had." Reaching out, she rubbed Amy's face. "One of the prettiest too."

"Thank you. I miss all of you. I will make a point of coming in to see everyone. And I will consider taking a shift over the weekends." She forced a smile. She swore her face might crack from the effort it entailed. Her legs were wobbling and her hands shaking. Grabbing the pudding, she exited the kitchen to find Glen waiting for her.

"I reckon it isn't necessary for me to share my surprise of seeing you out and about in town on a day other than the day Lola appointed for her ladies to do so. And I know you saw me, and you raced here for refuge." He stepped back and swung his hat toward the door indicating she should leave. He grinned broadly, but his eyes were void of any pleasantness. They conveyed danger. He frightened her. Lizzie was right. She didn't know him.

Somehow, she walked through the restaurant and into the lobby. There were many people around. She wished to stay. Being alone with Glen unsettled and terrified her.

"Come on, Amy," he urged.

Silly. Her fears were unfounded. As if he would hurt her. She scurried to keep up with him.

Outside, the bright sunlight struck her face and she stopped and stood blinking, waiting for her sight to adjust. Long fingers clamped around her upper arm, snatching her to him. Glen grumbled in her face, "No matter what measures I take to ensure you keep to yourself and out of sight and communication with the locals, you defy me."

She sputtered, "I don't know why you demand I do so. I came and got some bread pudding for Mr. O'Brien. It's his favorite. He always brings me the sweetest gifts."

His hold on her arm tightened and his hot breath smacked her in the face with each of his enunciated words. "I don't believe you."

"Excuse me, sir, but judging by Amy's face, you are hurting her." Jose. Her eyes finally functioned again, and she saw him standing to Glen's right. The lines in his handsome, angelic face were taut with challenge. "I suggest you release her."

"I suggest you go back to whatever pueblo you crawled out of. Amy is my wife, so mind your own damn business," Glen countered.

Before he hauled her away, she witnessed the disbelief and the disappointment in Jose's eyes. Her eyes filled with tears. She never wanted to hurt him. She definitely didn't want whatever started between them to end.

CHAPTER 5

RACHEL

*R*achel dutifully followed her mother and sister around as Sarah introduced them to her friends. They went to Sarah's old ranch to visit her sister-in-law Kate first.

The woman was expecting a baby and seemed quite happy about it. Apparently, from what Rachel could gather from the conversation, she and her husband had been married for several years and this was their first child.

Rachel couldn't believe how excited the woman seemed to be about living on a ranch rather than in town. Sarah had explained about how they had exchanged houses after Johnny died. Kate and her husband, Jim, took over the ranch and traded homes with Sarah. Rachel thought Sarah got the better end of that deal, even though her house was small.

Next, they went to the Big G Ranch, where Joshua had worked before he signed on with Conrad's oil company. It was quite a large operation. If she were inclined to be impressed by ranches, this one would do it. The women there were nice enough. Of course, Clara Mae was Conrad's sister.

They took tea together, and Rachel thought about how all of these women seemed content and happy with their lives, as her own sister, Sarah, did. Clara Mae and Laura were from the east. Rachel couldn't imagine they would prefer this life to the ones they had in Philadelphia. She shuddered as she thought of cooking, cleaning, and taking care of crying brats on a ranch, being tied to one man for all time. Well, she wouldn't have to worry about falling into that trap. Not her. She would be going back east as soon as she could manage it. Back to Aunt Mary, the parties, dances and social events. She would fill her dance card, bat her lashes, smile coyly and talk with one man, giving him hope, then move on to the next and do the same. That was the way to do it. Aunt Mary had the right idea.

"Rachel, how do you like our little town so far?" Clara Mae was asking her.

Rachel brought her attention back to the present and replied, "It certainly is not Philadelphia, is it?" She smiled and took a sip of tea, holding her cup daintily.

"Thank heavens for that," Laura said and the other women laughed as if she had said something wonderful.

Honestly, did the men out here brainwash these women or what? She had looked around to see if there were any handsome ranch hands about. The owners of the ranch were both married, though, so even if one or two of the hands were good looking, she would only tease them, never court them.

Next, they visited someone named Mary Catherine. Her mother-in-law was there too. The next day, it was Emma and Annabelle. They were married to Mexicans. She did enjoy speaking with Annabelle, though, and ordered several dresses from the young seamstress. Sarah had told her the woman had made both her wedding dresses. Rachel decided that as long as she was stuck out here in the wilderness, she might as well have some suitable clothing. Once she got back east, she would never wear them again.

A few days after that, it was time to move into the new house. Sarah helped Rachel and her mother unpack and arrange their things, and when the shipment arrived from back east, they worked on it. Soon, the house was clean and filled with the Lintons' items. The furniture the Browns had left mixed well with the things they had kept from their old home.

Rachel worked on her own bedroom until she had it just the way she wanted it, as close to her old room as possible. It would have to do until she could leave this wretched place. In the meantime, it would serve her well as her own private sanctuary.

One morning at breakfast, her father told her that he'd met one of the neighbors. "A Mr. Ryan. His wife passed a while back, and the house is too much for him to keep up, so he put it up for sale. Said he had an interested party but they wouldn't be moving in for a while. Rather than leave it empty, the new owner is allowing him to stay there but he will take care of the upkeep. Once a room opens up at the boarding house, Mr. Ryan will get a room there. Then I suppose the new owners will move in."

"That's very nice of the new owners to allow him to stay on for a while," Mrs. Linton said. "Did he tell you anything about them?"

"No, he hasn't met them. It was all handled through a third party."

"I see. Well, anyway, dear, what are your plans for the day?"

Mr. Linton replied, "Conrad has invited me to spend the day with him at his office. I believe he will also be taking me out to one of the drilling sites."

"How exciting. I'm sure you'll enjoy that. I've been invited to attend a meeting at the church. Some of the ladies get together there every Wednesday and make quilts," Rosella said. "They are going to teach me."

Rachel looked at her mother as if she'd lost her mind. *Quilts?*

"Rachel, darling, what are your plans?" her mother asked.

"I might read for a while, then I thought I would browse in some of the shops again."

"All right, but don't charge too much to my account," her father teased.

"Honestly, it seems that is all you do," her mother complained. "There is more to life than shopping. You need to take up a hobby or possibly even find part time work. I am sure there is something you could find to fill your time that is worthwhile, even if it is volunteer work."

"Work? Are you serious, Mother? What on earth would I do?"

"You love to read. Why don't you stop by the library? Sarah says there is a new one in town. Perhaps they need some help."

"I shall think about it, but I make no promises," she said to appease her mother.

When the breakfast dishes were cleared, both her parents left, leaving Rachel some time alone.

She wandered around the house, then went up to sit in her window seat to read. After a while, she looked out the window and watched the people walking around outside. It seemed the town was busy today. Men and women were hurrying from place to place. They all seemed to have a purpose. Rachel sighed. Maybe Mother was right. She needed a purpose to get her through the awful days until she could plan her trip back east.

Getting up from the seat in the window, she freshened up and then stepped outside. She looked both ways up and down the street before deciding to head to the shops first. If there was time left after shopping, she might stop by the library.

After browsing in Daisy's dress shop, she stopped in at the milliner's shop and found a hat to match one of the dresses Annabelle was creating for her. Since her father had opened charge accounts at all the stores in town, she told the clerk to put it on his account and then stepped outside the shop with her purchase. She was headed to the general store next. She looked around, choosing some candy for her sweet tooth and then went to the aisle that held soaps and perfume. She picked a few bars of scented soap before stopping to look at the tea choices. She was amazed at the many specialty teas available and picked up a few tins before going to the counter to charge the things she'd chosen.

When she walked out of the store, she nearly collided with someone. She looked up and saw Joshua Thomas.

He was wearing denim work britches, a denim work shirt with the sleeves rolled up, and as she looked down, she saw that he had cowboy boots on his feet. Atop his head sat a cowboy hat, which he tipped to her when he said, "Good afternoon, Miss Linton. Out for a day of shopping, I see."

"Yes, and why are you in town, Mr. Thomas? I would have thought you would be working. Should I tell my brother-in-law you are loafing on the job?"

He chuckled. "Well, you could, I suppose. However, your brother-in-law has sent me on some errands as he is showing your father around today."

So, now he was nothing more than a glorified errand boy. Cowboy, roughneck, and errand boy, when he could have had it all if only he had chosen to stay back east. What was wrong with all these people? It was as if they came out here and lost their minds. Was it something in the water? If so, she needed to get back home to Aunt Mary as quickly as she could!

"I won't keep you from your work then. Have a good day," Rachel said as she stepped aside.

"You do the same, Miss Linton." And then he went inside the store, leaving her on the porch shaking her head.

Oh, well, I'm not going to give that one another thought, she said to herself as she walked across the street to the tearoom. *He did look handsome, though. Those muscles! Must come from the outdoor work he does.*

When she got to the tearoom, she sat down with her packages and ordered a cup of tea and a slice of chocolate cake. While other girls had to watch their waistlines, Rachel could eat anything and still stay slim. It was the way she was built. She was tiny, like Aunt Mary. She was so much more like her aunt than either her mother or her sister. In so many ways, too, not just her size.

She was sipping her tea when she heard a deep voice say, "So, we meet again."

She looked up to see Joshua standing beside her. "Loafing again, I see," she replied as she took a sip of tea, dismissing him.

But the man would not be cast aside so easily. He was familiar with her haughty ways. "Mind if I join you?" he asked. "I thought I would grab a late lunch before I head out to the rig."

"Suit yourself," she said with a shrug.

"Thank you, don't mind if I do join you." He ordered a roast beef sandwich and a cup of coffee, then when the server left, he looked at Rachel again. "Did you get all your shopping finished and still leave your father with some money?" he asked.

"Not that it's any of your concern, but I did." She took a forkful of cake and placed it in her mouth.

"You are enjoying that chocolate cake," he commented.

"It is very good," she said. "You should try it."

"Nah, I never eat sweets during the day. After dinner, for dessert, is the only time."

Shrugging her shoulders again, she said, "You don't know what you are missing."

His lunch arrived then, so they were silent while he wolfed down a couple of bites. Then he wiped his mouth with his napkin and said, "The church is having a social Sunday afternoon, I hear. Will you be there?"

"I'm sure my parents will insist I attend. What does one do at a "church social" out here?"

His eyes sparkled with laughter. "There is plenty of food,

games to play, music, dancing. I think you will enjoy it. The ladies of the church auction off some of the quilts they have made to raise money for an orphanage near here."

"My mother is learning to make quilts with them. Today was her first day," she informed him.

"And you didn't wish to join them?" he asked as he finished his sandwich and took a sip of hot coffee.

"Well, sitting around with older ladies making quilts isn't something that interests me."

"You might be surprised to hear that many of the younger women take part in that activity as well."

"Why on earth would they do that? Oh, probably because there is nothing else to do here," she answered her own question.

"Miss Linton, I believe you would be surprised at the things there are to do here if you would just get to know some folks. There are plenty of young people in town."

"Hmm," was all she said. She had finished the cake and was pouring herself another cup of tea from the pretty flowered teapot the server had brought to the table.

"Back to the subject at hand. Will you accompany me to the church social?" he asked.

Rachel looked up at him in surprise. Why would she do that? She needed to keep her options open and accompanying Joshua might give people the wrong idea. They might think he had a claim to her. But then again, maybe it would spark the interest of some of the other young men in town to see her on the arm of one so handsome as Joshua Thomas. And she was sure it would make the other single girls positively green with envy. Decision made, she smiled her prettiest smile and said, "Yes, I would like that. Thank you for asking."

A bit surprised, Joshua hid it well when he said, "I will call for you at one o'clock then."

"I shall look forward to it. Now, however, I need to take my packages home and go back out. I have one more errand to attend to this afternoon."

"Why don't you allow me to walk with you and carry those packages before I head out to the ranch to check some things at the rig? I have a little time."

"Suit yourself," Rachel said as she waited for him to pull her chair out and help her up. She watched as he laid some money down to pay for both their orders and picked up her purchases, then she took the arm he offered and they walked out of the tearoom and down the street to her home together.

As they were strolling down the street in front of the hotel, Rachel noticed the same couple she had seen on her first day in town. Again, the man was rushing her along, but this time, she saw that the girl was dressed differently. She wondered what that was about. But Joshua was saying something to her, so she turned her attention back to him.

"And how are you settling in, now that you are in the house and all?"

"What? Oh, it's all right. It isn't home, but it passes for now."

"And what does that mean? I believe this is your home now."

"It doesn't seem like home to me. Philadelphia is what I know, not this place. But the house is nice. Mother and Sarah have fixed it up nicely, and we have some of our familiar old things here now. I've done my room just the way I like it. I have a nice window seat, like I had at home, where I can curl up and read or just watch the people passing by."

"Well, as time goes on and you make new friends, I'm sure this will become a place you fall in love with, just as I have."

I doubt that, she said to herself. *Besides, I won't be here long enough to make many friends. What would we have in common, anyway?*

She was relieved to see they had arrived at her house. She took the parcels from him and said, "Thank you for seeing me home. You'd probably better get back to work." She was glad of that, so she wouldn't have to invite him in.

"You are right on that. I do need to get going. I will see you at one on Sunday," he answered with a smile.

"Of course," she said.

When she got inside, her mother was home.

"How was quilting?" she asked.

"I enjoyed it. I see you did your shopping," Rosella said.

"Yes, let me show you the hat I got to go with one of the dresses Annabelle is making for me." She took the hat out of the box and her mother approved.

"You are right. It will match. I was happy you ordered new clothes to suit the area. I will have to place an order as well. What is in your other package?"

"Candy and tea from the general store. Oh, and a few scented soaps."

"Well, why don't we try that tea right now?" her mother asked.

"I, er, I just had tea at the tearoom, but I can have another." She followed her mother into the kitchen and sat down while the tea was brewing. They had chosen an English tea, which Rachel had been surprised to see. "They have a large selection of specialty teas at the general store."

"Is that right? I'll have to go have a look. Now, tell me about your day. Did you do anything besides shopping?"

"Well, I didn't make it to the library. I had planned to go back out after I brought my packages home, but it can wait until tomorrow."

Her mother nodded, not surprised to hear that her daughter had not gone by there. "Did you meet anyone at the tearoom or see anyone you've already met?" She got up to pour the tea.

"Mr. Thomas came in to have lunch. He, uh, he invited me to accompany him to the church social on Sunday afternoon. I told him I would. I hope that is all right."

"Of course, it is, dear. Joshua seems like a fine, hardworking young man. Sarah and Conrad speak very highly of him, and he was very polite on the train."

"Don't get any ideas. It is only one afternoon. We are not courting," Rachel said as she added two sugar cubes to her tea, stirred it and took a sip.

"Certainly, dear. I would not presume to get ideas where you are concerned." Her mother grinned into her cup.

When they had finished their tea, her mother went in to start dinner while Rachel went up to her room to put her new hat away and freshen up.

Over dinner, her mother informed her father about the church social. Of course, he, too, was delighted that Joshua would be taking her.

It's just one afternoon, she told herself again. *Soon, I'll be back in Philadelphia where I belong.*

The rest of the week went by very quickly. She did make it to the library. As it turned out, the woman who worked there told her she could very well use her assistance on Tuesdays and Thursdays. She even offered to pay her a small wage for her time. Rachel planned to hide that money away for her train ticket back east. When she had enough saved, she could wire her aunt and let her know she was coming to stay with her.

Finally, it was Sunday. Rachel attended church services with her family. Afterwards, they went back home where her mother fixed a late breakfast. They would have a late lunch/early supper at the social later.

Choosing a gray dress with pink lace trim to wear to the social, since it was one of her more simple dresses, she tidied her hair and put a pink bonnet on her head. Annabelle should have some of her new wardrobe finished soon, but until then, she was going to have to rely on her less fancy eastern dresses. She had been very observant of the other young women in town so as not to stand out in the crowd. Usually, she liked to, but here, she had no reason for it. It wasn't as if she was going to choose a young man and settle down here. This was a temporary bump in the road as far as she was concerned. But as she was stuck here for the time being, she might as well make the most of it. There was no harm in having a bit of excitement in her otherwise dreary life.

Joshua was right on time. She heard her father greet him from the hallway outside her room when she walked out the door. She took her time descending the stairs. It wouldn't hurt to make him wait a few minutes.

When she walked into the parlor, both her father and Joshua looked up. Her father smiled. "You look lovely, Rachel."

"Yes, you look nice. Shall we be going?" Joshua said as he stood up.

"Your mother and I will be along shortly. She is finishing up the food she promised to make for the meal." Her father stood as well.

Rachel gave him a peck on the cheek, then when her mother peeked her head in, she and Joshua both told her they would see her at the social.

The church was close by, so they walked. Several other of the townspeople were out and about, walking in the same direction. When they passed her sister's house, Sarah and Conrad were just coming out. Sarah was carrying a basket on her arm, her other one linked with her husband's.

"Well, hello, you two. Do you mind if we walk with you?" Sarah asked.

"Not at all. Join us," Joshua said.

"What is in the basket?" Rachel asked.

"I baked some bread yesterday to take to the dinner," Sarah said.

"It certainly smells good," Joshua said.

"She has slapped my hand several times for trying to steal a slice," Conrad said.

"Oh, you. I baked extra for you, and you know it," Sarah said with a giggle.

"Wait, you baked bread? When did you learn to do that?" Rachel asked.

"When I lived on the ranch. I cooked for the ranch hands and for Johnny, of course. Some, I picked up on my own, but a few of the other ladies in the area helped me learn to bake. I could teach you if you'd like," Sarah offered.

"Um, well, I'm going to be busy working at the library a few days a week. I am not sure I will have the time for baking," Rachel informed them.

"Oh, that's wonderful. And perfect for you as you love books so much," Sarah said.

Conrad and Joshua exchanged a grin. Maybe if she was working, the minx would stay out of trouble. Little did they know, trouble would find her sooner than they imagined.

CHAPTER 6

AMY

All the shame Amy suffered over the last few months did not compare to the shame she suffered as Glen marched her along the main thoroughfare. His strides were long and fast. Even if she didn't have tears pouring from her eyes and streaming down her face, she couldn't keep up. She stumbled multiple times, but he never slowed. He dragged her along, whether it be on her knees or her feet.

Recalling the pain in Jose's attractive face, generated more tears. He had been so kind to her. Kinder and more attentive than her husband. The very man who failed to find her for over a month after she arrived. The same man who hadn't spent but a few minutes with her on a couple of occasions before or after they married.

What had she done to deserve his wrath and neglect? It's not as if she would ever know. That required he engage with her—communicate with her.

Leaving the main road, he tugged her along to the less populated back lane and up to Lola's. Halting at the door, he circled and stared at her. "Good gosh. You look a mess." Fetching a handkerchief from his pocket, he held it in front of her. "Clean yourself up."

She sniffled. "I can't seem to do anything to please you."

"Amy, that's not true. I have a lot to prove, being an unknown and a newcomer out here. It's crucial my attention remains on that. And not on any trouble you make for yourself," he stated. His blue eyes had softened. He no longer appeared as threatening as before.

"Will you come inside? We can share a coffee together. Our cook is a wonderful baker," she pleaded.

The relaxed lines in his features and stance hardened again. "Did you not hear a word I just said? No, I can't stay for coffee or dessert. I am returning to the job site."

She started to ask why he left the site at all. Why had he been in town? But she thought better of it. Raising his hand, he knocked on the door. Hearing the lock turn, she sucked in a deep breath. The door stayed locked. Only those Lola approved could enter. "Here's your handkerchief. Thank you." She dangled it from her fingers at his side.

Again, he barely acknowledged her, his attention pinned on the door. "Keep it. I have others."

Naomi greeted them. Lola employed six women. Amy and Josie befriended one another. She had little interaction with any of the other ladies. Naomi happened to be one she rarely saw. A pretty brunette with a pouty mouth, and rather soft-spoken, Amy assumed she entertained her customers upstairs. "Mr. Chum..."she stuttered, and her eyes went wide in apology and alarm before continuing, "Mr. Jernigan, lovely to see you again."

The odd exchange had the hairs on Amy's arms and at the back of her neck prickling. Glancing at Glen, she witnessed a warning and an understanding in his gaze at Naomi. He insisted,

"Amy, go upstairs and rest. Soon, you will need to ready for the evening socializing."

Her legs didn't obey. Her feet stayed planted where she stood. Naomi and Glen stared at one another, unblinking. She swore they spoke to one another without speaking a word. Imposing on their strange and apparent personal encounter, Amy cleared her throat and reminded, "Have you forgotten how urgent it is for you to return to work?" She scrunched her lips, wrinkling her nose at him.

"I have not. Get upstairs," he responded.

Once you leave. Still, his eyes stayed on Naomi. "Perhaps you have changed your mind about coffee and pie," she pressed.

Her obvious defiance garnered his attention. Snapping his head in her direction, he barked, "No. I have not." Tipping his hat, he said, "Good day, ladies," and stomped off.

Waiting until she watched him walk out of sight, Amy went to go inside. Naomi blocked her way. Slapping her palm on the door, Amy forced it open wider and stepped through.

Halfway up the stairs, a slam sounded and echoed so loudly, Amy worried the vibrations might collapse the stairs. Grabbing the railing, she steadied herself and looked behind her. At the bottom of the steps, Naomi regarded her in evident contempt with her arms crossed under her chest. "Sorry if it startled you. The wind must have caught it," she insinuated before strutting away.

Her curiosity piqued and uncomfortable making any inquiries, Amy tried to rest. Unsuccessfully. Too many doubts, regrets, concerns, matters plagued her. After an hour of flipping from side to side and staring at the ceiling, she decided to draft a letter to her parents.

She had little success with it, either. After starting several, she abandoned the effort. Each one, she crumpled in her hand and threw aside. They all consisted of lies. Needless and selfish to worry her parents—she had nothing true to relay.

Even if Mr. O'Brien didn't show, Lola demanded all the women gather in the parlor room each evening. Dressed in a garish green and black corset better suited for a brunette and not a pale blonde, she joined the group downstairs. Surveying the room, she realized Naomi's absence. She wondered how often Naomi had attended.

Mr. O'Brien's face lit up when her eyes found him. Sitting on one of the sofas, a bouquet of lovely flowers bounced in his lap. "Mr. O'Brien, are those for me?" she purred, sashaying closer.

Averting his eyes and turning a scary shade of crimson, he replied, "You know they are. Nothing is as lovely as you, though."

"Shall we meet in the dining room? Dinner will be delicious, but I went out and got you a special dessert tonight," she suggested.

He chuckled. "You got something for me. A dessert." Standing, he handed her the flowers. "I can't imagine what you could bring for me... except yourself and delightful company."

Looping her arm under his, she guided him into the dining room. It astounded her each time she viewed it. The table adorned in expensive linens and silver along with the aromas permeating the room from the kitchen were worthy of the most wealthy, prominent individuals—even royalty. "We will call it a surprise."

Escorting Mr. O'Brien out after his usual two hour visit, with Virgil, Lola's hired heavy hand, on her heels prepared to diffuse any chargeable situation, movement outside of the illuminated area caught her eye. A figure from the darkness revealed himself. Jose. He came.

Her heart soared. He came. Swinging her arm to welcome him, Virgil brushed against her side and blocked her and any entrance. "State your business," he boomed.

Without pause, Jose approached the steps and farther into the lighted space. Unashamed and confident, he announced, "I wish to see Amy. If she won't refuse me."

Bouncing on her toes, she agreed to see him and yearned to do so, but Virgil didn't relent. "And you have the fee," he challenged.

"An entire week's worth," Jose stated. "I will call on Amy each evening."

Appeasing Virgil, handling the financial aspect, and restraining her impulse to throw her arms and hug Jose until he barely breathed were trying feats. Inside the library behind a closed door, allowed her the freedom to fulfill the one most important to her. Being a shorter man in stature, she wrapped her arms around his shoulders and his chin met her shoulder. Her face rubbed against his. The contact, though innocent and natural, generated an unexpected intimacy.

Reluctant to separate, but both sensing they should, they skittered about hesitating at one seat or another until they laughed. She fell into whatever support her bottom found. He withered to the floor, wiping at his eyes in unceasing laughter.

He spoke first. "You could have told me. About your husband. You can tell me anything."

Well, he shot from or for the gut. "I wanted to. I realize you believe I've deceived you."

"I do not. Your husband is not an honorable man. If not for you... I would've pulled my gun and killed him. Still can if you say he harmed you."

"No. No, Jose. No need for any bloodshed." They had things they needed to discuss. She couldn't ignore it, nor should she. But she could delay it. "Tell me about your day. Did you go to the creek? I'm dying to hear about the shenanigans the children got into today."

Moving from the floor, he took a seat across from her. He grinned and his eyes brightened. "I did join them at the creek.

They were on their way there after I left Lizzie's. I planned to go home and see if anyone needed help with any repairs or anything, but I couldn't resist." Jerking upright and slapping his thighs, he exclaimed, "You'll never believe what Eduardo did. The curiosity and fearlessness of a six-year-old astounds me. He ventured off upstream and found close to a dozen newborn copperheads."

Gasping, Amy blurted, more forcibly and louder than she intended, "Is he all right? Oh, my goodness, I would have fainted. I just know I would have."

Jose's eyes crinkled in the corners as he chuckled. "Of course, he is. I wouldn't ruin our evening by sharing an unhappy story. But you should have... I'm surprised you didn't hear Aunt Rosa. She raked Gabriela, her daughter and his mother, over the coals for not educating him on recognizing the difference between non-threatening and dangerous snakes."

"Oh no. I don't know, either. Not something we worried about in the cities back east," Amy admitted. "If I stay here, I'll try to remember to learn about them."

"Why wouldn't you stay?" he asked.

When he looked at her as he did, she couldn't imagine ever leaving. But she had made mistakes. A lot of them. And she no longer had any confidence to deem which were for the best—or the worst. "As much as I appreciate your friendship, we are both aware... both know..." She couldn't voice it. If she did, it became reality. She would rather savor the fantasy.

Planting his feet firmly on the floor, Jose rested his elbows on his knees and peered at her as if he understood and he too hated the truth. "It is because of your husband. You don't wear a ring. I suppose if you did, it would encumber your line of work. Which I am not judging," he insisted.

Of its own accord, her right hand blanketed her left. Her thumb and finger rubbed along the bare skin which had been adorned by a wedding band for less than two weeks before Glen asked for it, promising to keep it for her, the night he brought her to live and work at Lola's. She didn't feel married. She felt more alone than she ever had—except Lizzie needed her and Jose seemed genuinely interested in her as a friend and a woman. Glen behaved as if her well-being and reputation mattered none to him.

Sitting back in his chair, Jose relaxed, and the casual smile returned to his attractive mouth. She should not be staring at his mouth. But his lips were full, and his teeth were straight and very white against his tan complexion. "From what I recall from our conversation last night, you are an only child to furniture factory workers. Is it presumptuous of me to conclude you were not employed in the line of work you are now in? Lizzie is naïve to your situation. She believes you are working in an inn. I will not tell her differently."

He hadn't told her anything she hadn't already considered. Lizzie's focus had been anywhere except on Amy and her over-provocative outfit. Yet it shamed her to hear it. "Thank you," she replied.

"Are you in trouble? Let me help you. No respectable man would allow his wife to display herself and entertain gentlemen —no matter how innocent it might be." He dipped his chin and eyed her through his thick eyelashes.

"You claimed you weren't judging me. Your statements prove otherwise," she huffed. Tears burned her eyes. She bolted from her seat and went for the door.

Jose jumped out of his seat. His hands rested on her shoulders. Placing her forehead on the cool wood of the door, she shook her forehead into it.

He emphasized his concern and said, "I am worried about you. I am concerned for Lizzie. My instincts have never failed me. You are not only gorgeous, but you are loyal and kind-hearted. Just as Lizzie. It is not my intention to insert myself in someone else's marriage, but I can't ignore the nagging impression of you involved in a negative and potentially volatile relationship."

A few tears managed to escape from her eyes. "It is not you who is intruding on my marriage. My husband has unapologetically welcomed it. He ignores me completely. We have yet to consummate our marriage. He rejects any effort I make to spend time together in any capacity." The tears came faster, and her body shook with her sobs. "I have never felt so unappealing and discarded."

Squeezing her shoulders firmly, Jose twisted her around and slid his hands upward, cupping her face. "You are far from unappealing. And discarded." He chuckled. "The gentleman who left before I came in appeared to be floating on happiness. He, as I, would spend our last cent to have your attention and company. Dry your tears. Come and sit again. I will tell you the story of a wild horse my father bought. He forbade all of us from crossing the fence. I... had confidence I should not have."

Witnessing his sincerity and his dedication in redirecting her pessimism, she sighed and smiled. "I don't deserve your time or attention. Certainly not your money. You paid for a whole week. That's insane."

Taking her hand in his, he walked her back to her original seat and took the one across from her. "Never. Have I mentioned I have exceptional instincts?" he reminded.

Oddly, no one came and interrupted them. The hours went by and when one or the other began yawning, they decided to call it a night. Exiting the library, they found the downstairs dimly lit and silent.

"I will see you tomorrow evening. Same time," Jose stated.

"You can possibly come earlier as I don't have a regular scheduled, but probably best to wait," she replied.

Virgil stalked out the dark parlor room and loomed before them. "This is your only warning. In the future, if you require more from Lola's girls than the downstairs accommodates, a formal request must be made. And paid up-front."

"We engaged in nothing of the sort. We obviously got lost in our stimulating conversation. But… I will keep it in mind when I return tomorrow," Jose interjected.

Virgil appeared unappeased. Her confidence somewhat restored, a boldness ensued, and Amy countered, "If we weren't isolated in the library and could socialize with the other paying patrons, perhaps our visit would appear less questionable."

An admirable grin formed on Virgil's mouth before it vanished. "I will see to it. Have a good evening, Jose. And you, Amy, upstairs and rest."

The urge to dance a happy jig overwhelmed her. She resisted. But oh, how she yearned to partake in it. She had a man who showered her with compliments and non-judgment. The type of man she would need after she annulled her marriage to Glen. Knowing what she must do, and doing it, were two totally different things. She understood that.

Her sleep consisted of dreams. No nightmares, as they normally did. Except now her dreams were of Jose. Josie burst into her room and destroyed her pleasant slumber. "Up. Up. It's our day to do laundry. And Naomi is raising quite the ruckus over you."

Rolling onto her stomach, Amy groaned. "What is her problem? I don't ever see her. I can't fathom why she has any issue with me."

"Just get up. Come along. You and I can figure it out. Later," Josie persisted.

Naomi. Glen. Amy had her own reservations about them both. And the two of them. Throwing back her bedcovers and searching for her night coat, Amy defended, "I don't know her. We have never been in the same room together."

"Stop dawdling. She's with Lola now. Let us get to our chores and reduce any possible backlash," Josie prodded.

"I don't understand. There must be a reason. If Lola is listening, Naomi must have substantiation. Of some form."

Josie dropped to her knees and embraced her. "I'm so sorry. I honestly am. But Naomi came with highly regarded references. And with Lola, nothing will interfere with business. Doesn't matter who you are or what kind of person you are or what money you bring... she is connected in the big cities and will not cut those ties."

Any response eluded Amy. It's not as if she chose to be a part of the business. She certainly didn't need any future references. Out of bed and her face washed, she grabbed her laundry and started downstairs.

"I am sorry. I will always be your friend. I promise. You will discover that I am. I swear," Josie assured.

Amy lost interest in anything she said. She lost interest in anything except Jose and Lizzie. With them, she would have the friends she needed. She trusted it. She had to.

Scrubbing out her garments on the washboard and hanging them on the line, Josie stopped speaking. They worked. And Amy pulled out a handkerchief, the one Glen had given her. It had initials embroidered on it. N.C. *Naomi*. She'd referred to Glen as a Mr. Chum—

Who were they? Could it be he was not Glen Jernigan? Or was it her handkerchief? Women didn't carry handkerchiefs. Her head spun and she fumbled back and sat on the steps. Things continued going from bad to worst.

"And you will tell me about Lizzie. I sense something isn't right with her. I trust you, Amy."

CHAPTER 7

RACHEL

*T*hey arrived at the social and after Sarah had taken her bread to the appropriate place, the four of them walked around for a while, taking in all the sights and activities. Rachel had her arm linked with Joshua's as they made their way through the crowd. There were a few people she recognized, women her sister had introduced her to previously. It seemed they all had handsome husbands. Was she to assume that all the good men in the town had already been spoken for?

Of course, her escort was very good looking, although he wasn't what Rachel would consider to be 'husband material'. After all, he was just a laborer. A man who had given up wealth and civilization to live out here among the ranchers and roughnecks. A man who could have been working in a nice office back east instead of getting his hands dirty out here. As long as she lived, she didn't think she would ever understand these people who gave up the luxury of life back east to migrate to this godforsaken place called the Wild West. She certainly had not come by choice.

Even her parents seemed to be settling in quite well, which irritated her to no end. She had been hoping they would hate it and hightail it back home. But, no, they had bought a house, made friends, and her mother was even *quilting* with the church ladies, of all things. She would never have done that back home.

Since she was stuck here for a while longer, she might as well enjoy her day. She loved seeing the looks of envy as they passed by some young ladies who obviously wished they were the one walking with Mr. Thomas. This was like back home, when she used to bring out the jealousy in many a young woman when she had the eligible bachelors falling at her feet, vying for her affection. Rachel could get caught up in leading the young men on and making the girls envious of her here as well as back east. That would give her something to occupy her time until she could get back to Aunt Mary. And maybe she would make Mr. Thomas jealous while she was at it. Not that it mattered, of course, since she wasn't at all interested in him.

Yes, that would be quite entertaining, she thought as they sat down to listen to the music. Surprisingly, she really was having a good time. Joshua was very attentive to her, and she enjoyed being with her sister and brother-in-law as well. Soon, her parents arrived and joined them. After a while, she could see that her mother was liking this scene a bit too much. Her two daughters with handsome men, in a family style situation. And at a church function to boot. That simply would not do. Rachel had to put a stop to this before it went on much further. Her parents were too obvious in the fact that they would not object to Joshua Thomas courting their youngest daughter. Her parents had never approved of any of the young men who flocked around her back in Philadelphia. What was it about Joshua? Why, out here, he was a nobody. Of course, back home, he could be *somebody*.

Perhaps I can convince him to return with me, she thought and then shrugged off the idea. Something told her that wasn't his style. Running away with her to go back east, no, he wouldn't.

Soon, it was time for the meal, so she brought her thoughts back to the present as they all went to fill their plates at the lovely buffet that had been set out. She had to admit the food was very good. All the women had brought a dish for the potluck.

When they had finished eating, Joshua asked her to walk around with him to play some of the games and shop at the booths. She agreed and they set off. She noticed a couple of young men glancing her way a few times. She shuddered. They most certainly weren't her type at all, but they were not bad to look at. And they surely seemed interested in her. It might not hurt to do some harmless flirting with them later. It would be interesting to see how Joshua would handle that!

She threw darts at balloons at one of the booths after Joshua paid for her tickets. She didn't win anything but he succeeded in winning a small doll for her. It would look good in her window seat, she thought. She thanked him with a smile and they sauntered along to the next booth.

After a while, they sat down and he went to get cool cups of lemonade for both of them. Rachel was watching the activity around her when suddenly, the two men who had been stealing glances at her earlier appeared. One was red-haired, the other tall with dark hair.

"Well, now, seems you got rid of that dandy hanging around ye all day. What say you come take a walk with us now, sweet lady?" one of them said.

"You been givin' us the eye, now's time to make good on it," the other added. "And you are a new face in town, all the better."

"I beg your pardon?" Rachel replied sweetly. "I don't know what you mean."

"We seen ye lookin' at us behind your boyfriend's back."

"I surely did no such thing," she said, batting her lashes at them.

"I think the young 'lady'," the one with red hair said with a mocking tone, "needs a real man. Whaddya say we give her what she wants, Jeb, double?"

The dark-haired one, who must be Jeb, replied, "I think ye be right, Amos."

"I must ask you to move along. My escort will be returning soon," she said, suddenly becoming wary of the whole situation.

"Listen to that, Jeb, the lady be begging. She'll be beggin' all right, soon enough. Come on, girlie. Time to go."

"Ye be right, Amos. Best get going with her before the dandy comes back," Jeb said as he grabbed Rachel's arm.

"I say, stop that this instant. I am going nowhere with the likes of you!"

"Hear that, Amos, she got some fight in her. I like that."

"Hell yeah," Amos said as he grabbed the other arm and pulled Rachel to her feet. The next thing she knew, they were headed out away from the crowd, pulling her with them.

Rachel looked around for a friendly face but saw no one she knew close by. She tried to yell for help, but it was no use. Amos and Jeb were walking with her between them, but somehow they were making it look like she was going willingly, so onlookers weren't suspicious. When she tried to yell, Amos clapped a dirty hand over her mouth and whispered close to her ear, "Do that and ye'll get a lot more than ye bargained for, girl. When we's done with ye, we'll let our brothers have a turn, and there's three of them!"

Jeb laughed. "They all got big ones, too, just like us."

Amos chuckled. "Yeah, don't think you'll want them between your legs after you have Jeb and me. So best keep your trap shut, little girl."

Rachel didn't know what he meant by that, but she decided it was best if she didn't ask. For the first time in her young life, she was really frightened. Flirting had never gotten her into trouble back east. And all she had done was smile at them when she saw them looking at her, anyway. What on earth made them think they could treat her, Rachel Linton, refined eastern lady, like this? Where was Joshua?

Would he look for her when he came back with their drinks to find her gone? Or would he think she had abandoned him? Would someone tell him they saw her leaving with two men? Surely, he wouldn't think she went willingly, would he?

She looked around and saw that they were away from the others now and heading out to the far end of town. Oh no, how was she going to get away from these two *heathens*? Joshua wasn't looking so bad to her now.

JOSHUA RETURNED with the lemonade and when he didn't see Rachel on the bench where he'd left her, he looked around to see if she had wandered to one of the nearby booths. Not seeing her, he walked back toward where her family had been.

"Where's Rachel?" Sarah asked.

"I thought maybe she had come back here. I left her on a bench to get us some cool drinks and when I got back, she was gone," he explained.

Conrad and George exchanged looks. Conrad stated, "Maybe we should look for her."

The three men decided to go, and they told Sarah and Rosella to stay there in case she came back.

"Don't worry, I'm sure she just wandered around and lost her way back," Conrad told the women.

When they asked around, no one had seen a young girl fitting her description. Finally, one man said, "Hey, I think I did see a young girl with the Beecher brothers a while back. They were walking away from the social. Don't know what a girl like her would be doing with the likes of them, though."

"The Beecher brothers?" Joshua asked. He looked at Conrad who was as puzzled as he was.

"Who are they?" Conrad asked.

"Not a good sort. Family of five boys, all like the women a little too much if you know what I mean. Now, if a girl was with them, she was looking for something no good girl would if you get my meaning."

"Unless… she wasn't going with them willingly," George said. "Come on, boys, let's go. Which direction were they headed?" he asked the man.

"I'll go with you. You may need help if they took her back to their place." He motioned for some other men to go with them.

Since some of the men knew where the Beecher place was, they led the way.

"I saw Amos and Jeb at the social," one said.

"You know, there were two men watching Rachel a few times when we were playing games," Joshua said. "One was dark-haired and one had red hair."

"Yep, that's the Beecher boys, Amos and Jeb, for sure. Time's a wastin', men. We have to get to that girl before it's too late," the man who had been the most helpful said.

They hurried along, and suddenly, Joshua stopped and picked up something in the road. It was the tiny doll he had won for Rachel earlier. "Men, this is hers. I won it for her playing darts. She must have dropped it."

They all sped up then. When they got a little farther down the road, they heard a woman's voice saying, "Stop it! I will have you know that I am a lady. No lady should have to listen to the filth coming out of your mouths! Unhand me this instant."

"That's Rachel!" George said.

They approached the direction they heard the voice and then they saw her with the two men.

"A lady, huh? I saw how ye was lookin' back at us back there. Ye ain't foolin' me none. Ye was askin' for it. A good roll in the hay. And that's what we aim to give ye."

"This one's got some fire to her. I can't wait to tame it outta her," the other man said.

About that time, they saw Rachel knee him in the groin. When his brother slapped her, Joshua ran forward and landed a blow to his jaw that sent him reeling. As soon as he recovered from the shock, the fight was on. Pretty soon, the Beechers saw that they were outnumbered. Joshua grabbed Rachel and took her away from the fight. George was waiting for them.

"Rachel, are you all right?" he asked.

"Yes, Father, I am. They were vile creatures. They forced me to leave with them as soon as they saw Joshua leave to get our drinks. I told them I didn't want to go with them, but they forced me. They said they were going to do awful things to me and then share me with their three brothers when they were finished."

George hugged her and then he went to meet Conrad and the others, leaving her with Joshua. He meant to see the two men arrested. He left her in Joshua's care.

When he returned, he told them, "I am going to the sheriff. These men will go with me. Joshua, a word please."

Joshua, who was holding Rachel in his arms, soothing her, looked at her. "I will be right back."

Rachel nodded and he went to see what George wanted.

"Son, I know my Rachel, and I have no doubt that she was probably looking back at them when they were ogling her, thinking it was all innocent. Back east, the young ladies do that, but the young men are refined enough to know better than to pull a stunt like this. At least most of them. I'm sure I don't have to tell you that. Now, I want you to take Rachel home. Make her some tea, calm her down, let her freshen up. Then I want you to reiterate to her the dangers of what she did. Use whatever means necessary to make her see. Do you get what I'm saying, boy?"

Joshua nodded.

"I'm going to see the sheriff. The men back there are bringing those boys in. Then Conrad and I will let Sarah and Rosella know that all is taken care of. We'll give you plenty of time with Rachel at the house."

George and Conrad left to see the sheriff, the other men with the Beecher boys behind them.

"Come on. I'm going to take you home and make you some tea, let you freshen up. We can talk there," Joshua said to Rachel. He handed the doll back to her. "I think you dropped this."

"On purpose, hoping you would find it," she said as she took the doll and then his arm. "My father won't like it if you are alone with me in our home."

"On the contrary, he asked me to take you there and take care of you. He and Conrad are going to see the sheriff. The other men are bringing the Beecher boys in. They are the men who abducted you. Then Conrad and your father are going to go back to the social and reassure your mother and sister that you are all right. We will see them all a little later."

"Oh, I see," was all Rachel said.

When they got to the house, Joshua told Rachel to go freshen up. "I'll make us some tea while you are doing that."

"I do feel the need for a bath and change of clothes," she agreed as she went up the stairs.

Joshua chuckled to himself as he thought of the task ahead of him. He knew just how he was going to deal with Miss Linton, and he thought it had been a long time coming. And to know he had George's approval, made it just that much better.

RACHEL SANK into the tub full of bubbles and sighed. That was close! Who knew a smile could get a girl into so much trouble? Thank God Joshua and the others had found her in time.

Although, she was holding her own when they arrived. She shuddered to think what could have happened to her, though, as reality set in, and she started to cry.

By the time she had finished her bath and cried all the tears she had, she chose a different dress and steeled herself for the tongue-lashing she expected from Joshua.

When she got downstairs, he had the tea ready.

"I put a little something in yours to calm you down. Let's sit," he said as he carried the tea into the parlor.

She sat demurely across from him in one of the Queen Anne chairs her mother had sent from the old house back east. He was seated on the settee.

He handed her a cup of tea and sat back to enjoy his. Finally, he said, "Tell me exactly what happened, Rachel, before we rejoin the others."

"I-I am not going back to the social," she said.

"I didn't say we had to, but your family will join us later. Now, I want to hear, in your words, what happened today."

"I was sitting on the bench waiting for you when the two men approached me. They said some things and asked me to come with them."

"What did they say?"

"I don't remember all of it. Something about noticing that I saw them watching me and I was watching them too. Joshua, I smiled at them. That was all. It meant nothing."

"Apparently, they thought it meant something. Rachel, that may be the way young ladies conduct themselves in the social circles of Philadelphia, but out here, some of these men don't understand that it means nothing, like the men back east. Do you understand what I'm saying?"

"I told them I wasn't going with them, but then they forced me to. They told me if I screamed, that when they were through with me, they would give me to their brothers and that I wouldn't want that." She ignored what he had said.

"Rachel, come here, now," he commanded softly, setting his cup on the table.

"What? Why?" she asked.

"Because, you, young lady, need a stern lesson in proper behavior."

"Who do you think you are? My father will be here soon. I will tell him what you said and he will forbid you to see me again. Is that what you want?"

Joshua chuckled. "Your father gave me his blessing to do what I deemed necessary to instill in you the proper way to conduct yourself with men."

"You are lying! My father would never—"

"Oh, but he did, my dear Rachel. And he will keep your mother and sister away long enough to give us time to sort this out. Now, are you going to come to me, or do I have to come get you? I can promise you if that is the case, it will go much harder on you."

"W-what are you going to do?" she asked as she took a big gulp of the whiskey-laced tea for courage.

"You'll find out when you get over here. I am going to count to three. One."

"All right. All right." She got up and walked slowly toward him. When she got close enough, he pulled her across his lap.

"This is ridiculous, scandalous, improper!" she exclaimed as she kicked her legs.

"No, it isn't, and it's long overdue," he countered as he pulled her dress up over her back.

"Y-you can't do that!"

"Yes, I can. I will leave your bloomers on. But you, young lady, are going to get a spanking. One that should have been given long ago."

Rachel couldn't believe her ears. Just who did he think he was? Her own father had never laid a hand on her. And she didn't believe for one minute that he had given Joshua permission to do so. This man was not her beau, her betrothed, or her husband. He was out of line.

But she was in no position to argue those points at the moment, because he was holding her legs down with his own and with one hand, he grabbed her wrists and held them behind her back. Then, with the other hand, he began peppering her bottom with hard smacks, first on one cheek and then the other. Rachel tried to kick but it was no use. His hold on her was too strong.

As he smacked, he started to lecture. Something she truly hated! "Now, from now on, you will not look at men with a wink or a smile. You will not bat your eyes at them or flirt in any way. You are a lady, and if you intend to remain a lady, you will act like one. The social circles of Philadelphia are much different than the Wild West. The sooner you realize that, the safer you will be. Am I making myself clear?" he asked.

"Men out here are heathens," she argued. The spanks hurt, but they somehow felt right to her. She must be losing her mind after the day's events. That was the only logical explanation for the way she was feeling right now.

The smacks started to rain down harder at that outburst. "Rachel Linton, listen to me. Yes, some, like the Beecher boys, are heathens. Most are not. But there are more men than women. Men hunger for the feel of a woman out here. That's why there are so many mail-order brides. When a girl or a woman acts the way you did today, it gives the men the wrong idea. I know it is a game back east, but the men in your social circle there are aware of it. Here, you cannot and must not do anything to give a man or anyone else the idea that you want more than a mild flirtation. It isn't done. At least not by ladies. Now, a woman who works in a brothel, yes, but you are not like that."

He never let up on her poor burning bottom. Even through her bloomers, she felt every slap his hand laid on her. It stung, it hurt, it humiliated her. But his words hurt even worse. When she finally began to sob and fell limp across his lap, with no fight left in her, he stopped.

Then he did something surprising and lifted her up and into his arms. He cradled her against his chest and spoke softly to her. "Rachel, honey, I don't want you to get hurt. It would have killed me if those men had succeeded in having their way with you. I care what happens to you. I know you don't think I'm good enough, but this isn't Philadelphia. You forget that I came from the same social set you did. I know what girls in your position want. And a roughneck isn't it. I like your company. I only wish you liked mine as well."

"I-I do like your company. B-but, someday, I am going home."

"You really think your father will allow that?" he asked, surprised.

"I am not a child!" she argued.

"Rachel, you need to give this town and its people a chance. Haven't you met a lot of good people already? Most are not like those men today."

"I don't like it here," she said between sniffles.

"You will learn to love it, as everyone else who comes here does."

"I doubt that."

"All right. We can talk about that another time, but for now, go wash your face and tidy your hair. Your family will be back soon." He kissed her forehead.

She hurried up from his lap and scurried away to have a few minutes alone before she had to face the others. Would they know what Joshua had done to her? She washed her face and fixed her hair, smoothed her dress and calmed herself before walking back downstairs.

"Could I please have a cup of plain tea with sugar before they get here?" she asked sweetly.

"Of course, you go sit and I'll bring it in. There is more in the pot and it's still hot."

They were sipping tea and talking quietly when her parents returned, Sarah and Conrad with them.

Her mother ran to her. "Oh, Rachel, are you all right?"

"Yes, Mother, I am fine," she said. "We've been having tea and talking about the differences between Philadelphia and here."

Sarah and Conrad looked at each other. Joshua winked at Conrad.

George spoke up. "The Beecher boys are behind bars for now."

"Well, is anyone hungry? I can make some sandwiches for supper," Rosella offered.

"I'm still full. I ate too much at the potluck," Conrad said.

The others agreed, so she went in to make a fresh pot of tea for everyone instead.

"I should go if I'm going to be at the site at sunup in the morning," Joshua said as he stood. "Rachel, will you walk me to the door?"

She got up, to the amazement of the others, and joined him.

When they got to the door, out of sight of the others, he pulled her to him. "No hard feelings?" he asked.

She shook her head. "I-I understood what you said. I just didn't realize it before today. I thought it would be entertaining to tease them a little."

"Now, you know better, right?"

She nodded.

"You know I would never hurt you intentionally, right?" He leaned down to kiss her forehead again.

Rachel felt butterflies in her stomach. She thought it was because it had been a stressful day. But when he kissed her lips, she knew that wasn't the reason. Something stirred deep within her. The touch of his lips on hers was fascinating, like nothing she had ever experienced before. It did funny things to her. And, yes, she did know that he would never hurt her intentionally, not like those men today had done.

"I have to go. I'll see you soon. Please behave. Promise me," he said as he opened the door and stepped out onto the porch.

"I promise," she said. She shut the door behind him and stood for a moment, her finger on her lips before she went back to the parlor. She excused herself, saying it had been a long day and she wanted to go to bed.

"Goodnight, dear," her mother said in a worried tone.

"Sleep well, Rachel. I'll check on you tomorrow," Sarah said.

Her father and brother-in-law also told her goodnight.

In her room, alone in bed, she thought about everything that had happened. It was like Joshua was her knight in shining armor, her Prince Charming, coming to her rescue. What on earth was wrong with her? She couldn't get involved. She was going back east. Wasn't she?

CHAPTER 8

AMY

$\mathcal{T}$rembling on the steps with the mystery handkerchief in hand, even in her drabbest moments she nor anyone could escape the assail of Lola's excessive perfume. Her eyes watered and her nose itched. Bouncing up, Amy staggered and faced her employer.

One of Lola's eyebrows lifted and wriggled before dropping again. "Amy, please join me in the library," she stated.

Scenarios raced through her mind. If Naomi accused her of breaking any 'house' rules, Amy could in return accuse Naomi of —something. There must be something. Or she could accept whatever blame the other woman pinned on her and tolerate Lola's verdict. Could she, though? If she didn't, where would she go? The answers she craved would probably be lost to her.

Swallowing past the lump in her throat and possibly any ounce of pride she had, Amy followed Lola. Josie's hesitant voice assured, "I will finish your laundry. Don't you worry about it."

Lola led her to the library. Entering, Amy didn't see Naomi. It surprised her to find Virgil sitting in one of the reading chairs. He stood and waited until both women were seated.

Sighing, Lola peered at her in silence. It seemed like an eternity before she spoke. "Do you and Miss Naomi have issues with one another?" she inquired.

She received an opportunity to defend herself. Sort of. Against what, she couldn't imagine. She shook her head and avowed, "Not that I am aware of. I rarely see her. I barely recall seeing her in the evenings socializing. Unless she attended the previous two evenings while I entertained Jose... Mr. Gonzales in the library, and still, she and I have shared no interaction."

Narrowing her right eye as if in deep contemplation, Lola admitted, "I believe you. But, because Naomi has issued a formal charge against you, I cannot overlook it and I certainly won't refuse appropriate action be granted."

Amy's hands trembled. She buried them in the folds of her night coat and slid them under her thighs. The shuddering relocated to her shoulders and chin. Her muscles tightened and quivered. The spasms in her face mortified her. She wouldn't cry.

Closing her eyes and mumbling something inaudible, Lola reopened them, and a visible empathy appeared and calmed Amy. Patting a place beside her on the sofa, Lola stated, "Come and sit beside me. I hate I have upset you. I truly do detest it. But over the years, out of necessity, I have developed a heightened knack for distinguishing the good apples from the bad. My hands are tied with Naomi, but there is slack in those binds."

Even concentrating as hard as she could, Amy had no comprehension of the matter at hand. "I apologize if I have violated any of your guidelines or disrespected you in any way. I am grateful for the opportunity you have given me." She rose and sat beside her employer.

Lola cocked her head quickly and laced their arms together, interweaving their fingers. "You have done no such thing. I recognize a false allegation when I hear it. And to save us all from additional angst, I will not share any more of it with you. We all live under the same roof. We all hope to remain here. So, Virgil and I have spoken and from tonight forward, you and Jose can and will meet in the dining area or the parlor. We see no need to segregate the two of you. It only provides others with enough suspicions and whispered grievances until unfounded allegations are introduced."

Had she heard Lola correctly? Virgil claimed he would see to it that she and Jose gained approval to visit in the main rooms, but she doubted he would gain Lola's consent. Being called in to meet with her about a complaint crushed any lingering hope she had. Daring a glance at Virgil, she caught sight of his fleeting wink. Taking a deep breath, Amy directed her focus on Lola. "Thank you. I am extremely appreciative of your generosity and in your trust in me."

Lola squeezed her hand over Amy's and rolled her eyes. "You have given me no reason not to. And I suggest you don't." She smiled and continued, "After you leave this room, you are not to speak of our conversation with anyone. I've concluded we have one instigator among us and don't wish for any others to jump on her wagon. I've arranged for you to meet with our seamstress tomorrow at noon. You've done well for yourself here. You've made quite the impression on Mr. O'Brien, Mr. Ramsey, and Mr. Gonzales. Enough that they are regulars. And Mr. Ramsey is not easy on the eyes and even less easy to please. Yet you've managed, and you deserve clothing of your own... not something I've passed down to you."

Amy couldn't believe her amazing fortune. Having Lola and Virgil as advocates on her behalf, opposite of Naomi, supported what she deduced—the woman shouldn't be trusted. And it required she watch her back. It necessitated she diligently maintain a heightened sense of awareness.

Offering her thanks again, she left the library to return to her laundry. Realizing she still had the handkerchief Glen gave her folded in her right hand, she started to rid herself of it, but thought better of it. She had proof. Proof of what, she had no idea.

⁓

MEETING with an honest to God seamstress and having garments fitted to her exact measurements exhilarated and humbled her. Expensive clothing didn't assuage her shame. Nothing could. Besides the fact the colors and cuts were revealing and gaudy. Maybe they were exactly what she should own and wear. She dreamed of a man other than her husband. How dare she ignore truth. She lived and earned wages in a house of ill repute. It couldn't be denied. She lived in the life... she adopted the life.

She had a husband. A man her father had also corresponded with and believed him to be a decent Christian and a suitable husband for her. Her parents assumed she left them, married, and lived an honest life. She could make the argument that she didn't lie or steal from anyone, but she couldn't claim she lived honestly. As if she could ever advise her parents of her thoughts of annulling her marriage. Then again, if they learned of her current living and employment situation it wouldn't be so outrageous. Now, would it? A woman capable of offering herself in any form to a man before marriage and certainly afterward to a man other than her husband as she had, whether or not sexual favors occurred, would be apt to dally in a multitude of heretical actions.

But not her. She took vows. Instead of allowing her mind to run amok, she must speak with Glen. Unfortunately, he only came to the Parlor on Saturday. Any consideration she gave to requesting Jose cease visiting her caused her stomach to hurt. Why ask him to stop coming and not her other regular patrons?

Because he made her laugh. She enjoyed and craved more of his touch. He genuinely appeared to care for her and delight in her company. And Glen did not.

Lost in her thoughts as she walked along on her way back to the Parlor, the mention of a church social in several conversations reached her ears and penetrated her consumed conscience. The perfect opportunity to appear with her husband and begin her transition back into the community. She couldn't wait to speak with him Saturday. The time had come for them to begin a married life together. It could only be a positive decision. It would rid her heart, mind, and body of anyone except him if they did. She prayed to reconnect with the few friends she had when she first arrived.

Quickening her pace, she hurried inside and upstairs to tell Josie about the social and her determination to speak about it to Glen and pressure him to step up. The doubting him and the aloofness in their relationship must end. The negative effects were detrimental to her... him... and them.

Pulling items out of the bottom drawer of her bureau, her back turned to Amy, Josie's shoulders shook as Amy confided in her. The subsequent outburst came as no surprise. Circling, clutching her abdomen, and staggering into a chair, she laughed until she cried. "I am sorry. I honestly am sorry. But there are so many wrongs in your plan. There is nothing right in it," Josie explained.

Bewildered and embarrassed, Amy responded, "I don't understand. It's unflawed."

Huffing, Josie cocked her head. "It may be. Your husband on the other hand is anything but."

Disappointed, Amy sat at the foot of the bed facing the door, placing Josie behind her and hopefully shielding her disappointment. "I don't know why you would say such a thing. You don't know him."

The bed sank and arms came around hugging her. "Oh,

honey. I know men. I can interpret their wants and needs before they can. And your husband has his best intentions at heart. Not yours," claimed Josie. "He won't be escorting you to some simple church social. And you need to behave as the independent woman you are. And accept reality. Once you walk inside Lola's doors, you will never be socializing with anyone outside again. We are tainted. And though a number of the local women are thankful we are here as it alleviates them of the tasks they deem foul and uncomplimentary, we will never be acknowledged and allowed inside their idealistic existence."

She didn't want to confront reality. Things could be different. They had time. She realized the longer she continued in her current role, her chances of returning to her previous status dwindled. And her intuition expected Glen would persist in his stance that she remain at Lola's.

Every word Josie spoke, Amy hated. Because she recognized their truth. Especially the independent woman part. Enough. Amy would attend the social. One way or another.

Feigning a headache, she left Josie and went to her room. Waiting until Saturday to voice her appeals to Glen would be challenging.

Wednesday night, Jose arrived at his usual later hour. She didn't have a scheduled visitor on that night. Except Jose. Several newcomers had come. And one, in particular, had taken a liking to her. Grateful to see Jose come through the door, she excused herself from the new patron and greeted Jose.

"As happy as I am to see you... go back to your customer. This is my first time invited into the actual parlor. I will wait to capture your attention until later. Garnering any unwanted or unhappy reactions will hinder such," Jose insisted.

Hours later after entertaining everyone and impressing her new client, Mr. Echols, with her singing, Naomi joined the gathering. Again, it dawned on Amy she saw little of the woman. The woman who seemed to be acquainted with Glen. The very one who issued a complaint against her.

Swooping inside the room and fanning her arms and massive aroma of a sweet perfume, she nudged Mr. Echols in the shoulder with her hip. Yes. She hiked her leg and planted her shoe on the bench beside him. He slid over and she hoisted herself over the piano and stretched out across the top on her belly. Her small, but lovely breasts heaved out of her corset. Making an inaudible tune request, at least to Amy it was as the explicit scene had her neck and face heating until she retreated into a corner, Naomi raised and stiffened her chin and glowered at her.

The petite brunette serenaded her audience in a song about love and lust unfamiliar to Amy. She wanted to find fault with it. She could with the content or at least in the innuendos, but not with the performance. Naomi had a sultry, mesmerizing voice. She also had the corresponding appearance and attitude to encourage it.

After the song, she provocatively climbed off the piano. Every man in the room, except Jose, extended their arms containing substantial cash. She gathered the money, flirted with the benefactors, and brushed into Amy as she went to leave. "Money is everything. Nothing can or will ever compare."

Speechless, Amy watched her strut upstairs. She suggestively waved and crooned a few verses of another bawdy song.

"Don't overthink her, Amy. She's jealous. That's all. Nothing more," Jose stated.

He didn't know about the incidents between the two women nor her suspicions surrounding Glen and Naomi. Or the official complaint Naomi made against her. But did he have insight into the true issue? Or enough perception to counter what she lacked?

The two of them never had the chance to converse privately. Both, she believed, were unnerved at the abrupt contrast that came from being isolated to the library to thrust into a room with others. They mingled with the other guests. She sang again. As if any performer would choose to follow Naomi. But after an incredible amount of persuasion and cash presented, she agreed. Jose's attention and admiration inspired her. "Get back in the saddle, Amy. She is memorable. You, more so."

Thursday came and went. Mr. Ramsey brought her a beautiful hair comb and scented soaps. He apologized if the soaps were inappropriate and insinuating as he meant no offense. She kissed him on his forehead and cupped his face. Smiling and gazing into his one eye, she assured him she thought his gifts were wonderful and thoughtful. She knew the other girls avoided his attention and detested being the object of his affection, but Amy found him charming. And sad. He told her how his wife left him after his accident. She couldn't bear to look at him with his eyepatch and scarred face. She claimed the hand with the missing fingers gave her nightmares. It certainly said more about her than him. His appearance had changed, but his soul had not. And he had a good one.

Because of her responsiveness to Mr. Ramsey, she wondered if he would ever leave. He stayed much longer than usual. Jose played cards for hours with the other waiting callers. She and he shared eye contact and smiles throughout the evening.

Due to the late hour, both she and Jose were yawning as they sat together and talked. He showered her with compliments and had her laughing, relaying the daily stories of his nieces and nephews. When he announced his departure, a surge of loneliness stormed her. All her problems disappeared in his presence. She felt invincible and protected during their meetings.

On Friday evening, the noise and activity at the Parlor were excessive. Cigar smoke funneled around their heads escaping through the archways and throughout the establishment. The men taunted one another as one card game ended, and another began. Lola sat in her regular seat smirking as she observed the abundance of patrons and the profits pouring in.

Jose arrived as Naomi sashayed down the stairs whistling a melody. The rooms went silent. She suggestively paused and posed and the sequins on her corset glistened as they sporadically caught light. Tinkling of piano keys accompanied and were interposed when her whistling ceased. Amy found the entire exhibition mesmerizing. Naomi knew how to captivate a crowd.

All eyes were on Naomi. Glancing at Jose, he too was spellbound by the performance. Naomi moved through the audience touching and engaging the men as she sang and swayed. She received boisterous applause and compliments at the end.

Stepping over to Jose, it shocked Amy how exhausted he appeared. His eyes were heavy and dull.

"Amy, I can't stay. I didn't want you believing I would miss any opportunity to be with you, but between working at the drill site, tending the crops, the livestock, and seeing you... I am in dire need of sleep," he informed.

It surprised her that he began working at the site. He told her he interviewed, but he never said another thing about it. "I didn't know you started with Mr. Appleby's company."

"I did a few days ago. I am doing my best to make a great impression and keep up with my duties on the farm. I have an early morning in the crops. Allow me to get some rest and I will see you tomorrow." He gazed at her in apology and appeal.

Placing her hand in his, she nodded. "Of course. Until tomorrow." She had no reason to doubt him. But what if he and Glen had been in contact and it impacted his decision to limit his time with her. Then again, why would it? Glen didn't care who she kept company with. Except for anyone related to the Big G. But the drill sites were on Big G land. Tomorrow, she would see her husband. She intended to obtain his attention, have him attend the social with her, and put all her fears to rest by claiming him and living together as the married couple they were.

FINALLY, Saturday came and Glen didn't disappoint. He showed before any guests did. Standing in the foyer, he placed his palm out. She pretended not to notice. "Come sit with me. I would like to discuss something with you," she stated.

His eyes were everywhere but on her. "No time, Amy. Hand over your earnings this week. I hear you have acquired another regular that paid for an entire week. And that Lola had a full house last night."

She swore the heat coursing through her body resulted from the boiling of her blood. An uncontrollable anger surfaced within her. "I believe you can grant me some of your time. I am after all your wife."

Grabbing her wrist, he pulled her into the dining area. "What has come over you? Is it your monthly? Bring me my money."

"It is not 'your' money," she growled.

"The hell it ain't. As my wife, you have work outside of our home because I allow it."

"Outside of our home... what home?" she challenged.

His gaze hardened and the fury she observed in it had her step away from him. Releasing her wrist, he removed his hat, dropped his head and ran his fingers through his hair. Shaking his head, he raised it and he appeared less frightening. "I'm sorry. It's been an extremely long week. There have been some issues at the site. Regardless, I should not behave so."

"We both need a little fun. Tomorrow, there is a church social. I would be thrilled if we went. Imagine how enjoyable it will be. I heard there are games and auctions and food. We can mingle with your co-workers who will eventually be our neighbors and friends," she urged. He didn't have to speak a word. She witnessed his rejection. He sighed. His shoulders dropped. And he refused to look at her. "Why not? I'm tired of waiting for us to begin our lives together. It took over a month for you to find me. Then you rushed us to marry. For what?"

Chewing his bottom lip, he reminded her, "You work in a parlor house. No upstanding citizen... well, woman, will give you the time of day."

Her eyes filled with tears. "Maybe they will. You placed me here. It's only been a few weeks. Perhaps no one knows. We can at least try."

"No, we can't. Please be patient with me a little bit longer. Go on and fetch the money." His fingers clamped onto her shoulder. He squeezed them and patted her shoulder before swinging his head toward the stairs.

She did as he requested. The sooner he left, the better. She could escape to her room and surrender to her pain. Every part of her hurt.

It took multiple attempts by Josie to coax her from her bed. Advising her that Lola inquired about her absence and threatened to come get her proved successful. An emptiness seized her. A numbness. She had enough money to return home. What other option did she have?

Jose stood waiting at the foot of the stairs. He came early. Glimpsing her, his eyes brightened, and a gigantic smile spread from one ear to the other. "Are you unwell?" he asked.

"I suppose I am," she replied.

He took her hand in his and guided her to the sofa. "Sit and tell me what is troubling you."

"No. I would rather you tell me about your day and the kids." She would not let her troubles dampen their evening. If she told him she decided to return home, would he object? She certainly didn't have the strength to deny him if he did. But Glen reiterated what she already knew. In Oklahoma, she would never be anything other than a scorned woman.

She wished it would never end. Jose's casual touches. His

wonderful stories. His lively eyes and engaging smile. Her hands were tied. She had no choice.

As their time came to an end, he peered into her face. "You don't trust me," he declared.

"Of course, I do. You have given me no reason not to," she emphasized.

"I know something is troubling you. You can confide in me tomorrow night. Lizzie has been unwell most of this week. She isn't aware I have been visiting you, but she asked me to get a message to you. It made little sense to me, but she requires the alternative. Is this about the medicine you sent to her? I would agree it did little to alleviate her ailing as she has remained inside her home. Floyd hopes she feels well enough for the social tomorrow."

"Are you going?" she blurted.

He shrugged. "I, nor my family have attended any. We have our services on the farm. It is my understanding the social is open for all to enjoy. Do you plan on going?" he inquired.

I do now. "Yes. Glen declined to take me, but I do wish to go."

His lips parted, revealing the bright white of his teeth. "I would be honored to spend a beautiful afternoon with you. Let's plan to meet there. I will not chance sullying your reputation if we arrive together. I definitely won't miss this opportunity, though. We will present it as a chance meeting at a public event."

She believed she could burst from happiness. Throwing her arms around his neck, she whispered in his ear, "Thank you. Thank you. You can't imagine how happy you make me."

Between the preparations, recruiting Josie, and the exhilaration, she didn't sleep a wink. Pulling out one of her dresses, a simple garment her mother sewed, she shook it out and laid it on the bed. Josie disapproved of the whole idea but promised to aid in her leaving the house undetected.

It all went off without a hitch. Jose waited on her exactly as he said he would. He bought her some peanuts. They played a few games. It felt amazing to be out and about with other towns-people and in the company of Jose. It gave her hope. She could return to a 'normal' life.

They crossed paths with Lizzie and Floyd. Lizzie looked terrible. She had dark circles under her eyes. The paleness of her skin highlighted them. Guiding her over to a table containing quilts, Amy asked, "The elixir didn't work?"

Lizzie's voice sounded weak. "It did not. It has made me incredibly sick." Grasping Amy's hand, she continued, "Will you still help me? I beg you."

"Yes. Yes. Tuesday at seven in the morning. Meet me in front of the hotel." Nothing good would come of this. Her chest tightened. They were making a huge mistake.

"Thank you, my sweet friend. You look beautiful. It's wonderful to see you out and about and happy. I am relieved Glen is responsible for the stunning smile on your face."

"Lizzie, I hate to rush you along, but let's finish up so I can get you back to bed," Floyd pressed. He and Jose stood behind them carrying on their own conversation.

Amy didn't have the heart to tell Lizzie it was Jose not Glen responsible for making her happy. Lizzie had been right about Glen. Once they had the nasty business behind them, Amy would confess it all to her friend.

Strolling around the table and booths, she and Jose walked up behind a couple walking arm and arm. The woman had her head resting on the man's shoulder. Amy wished she and Jose could be openly affectionate. She wished she were unmarried, and they could be affectionate and pursue an honest relationship.

The dark-haired woman darted to a game booth on their right. All the breath left Amy's body. Naomi. She had her usually loose hair plaited down her back. She didn't reek of heavy perfume. Her lips were natural, and she too wore an ordinary dress. The man swerved to follow her. Glen.

CHAPTER 9

RACHEL

*R*achel spent the next few days becoming acclimated to her part-time position at the local library. She was surprised to find that she actually enjoyed the time she spent there. Mrs. Richards, the librarian, was a pleasant woman, middle-aged.

She hadn't seen Joshua since the social and of that, she was almost sad. Almost. She couldn't become attached to him. Why, he wasn't the right man for her at all. A laborer? No, not in this lifetime. Besides, she was going back east soon.

On the other hand, she thought about how he had come to her aid. Then she remembered his hard hand on her bottom. She ought to be appalled. But she wasn't. In fact, after the pain went away, she had felt... well, relaxed, even excited. *That is preposterous*, she chided herself. And if that was the way the men out here treated their women, the sooner she got back to Aunt Mary, the better. Honestly!

She really should send a wire to her aunt soon, letting her know to expect her. But she didn't want her sister or her parents to know until she was well on her way, so that would have to wait. In the meantime, she could fill her time with her work, reading, and being the dutiful daughter. It was certainly a quieter life than she was used to. Was she bored, though? One would think she would be, but somehow, she wasn't.

One evening at supper, her sister and brother-in-law joined them. Sarah asked if she'd like to stay with her for a few days as Conrad had to go to Oklahoma City.

"For work," he explained. "Joshua will be accompanying me."

Rachel was surprised to hear that. After all, wasn't he a roughneck? Why on earth would the boss take him with him on a business trip? "Why, may I ask, are you taking one of your roughnecks with you?" she asked boldly.

Conrad chuckled. "You are nothing if you are not direct, sister dear. Joshua is learning the business and it will be good for him to see what goes on with bigger companies. I am meeting with the company that helped me get started."

"I see," Rachel replied, although she really didn't see at all. Turning to her sister, she said, "I would love to stay with you. It would be fun, just like the old days back home."

"That's what I was thinking too. Come by Thursday after you finish at the library."

"I don't work again until Tuesday after that. When will Conrad be home?" she asked.

Conrad answered her question, "Joshua and I will return on Monday evening, so that works out well. You and your sister will have the entire weekend together to do girlie things."

"Girlie things?" Rachel mocked.

"Oh, Rachel, stop," her mother said. "You know what he means."

Her father and Conrad were laughing by now.

Sarah ignored them and said, "That's right. We can stay up late, eat cookies, go shopping, whatever you want to do, within reason, of course."

After supper, she and Sarah cleared the dishes while their mother served dessert. When their guests had gone home, Rachel excused herself.

"Rachel, why do you tease Conrad so?" her mother asked as she headed to the stairs.

"I wasn't teasing him. It just sounded funny when he said girlie things." She giggled and went on up to her room to the sound of her mother adding, "Do not give your sister any problems this weekend."

Really! What sort of problems would she give her sister? Did no one have faith in her? She could be good when she wanted to be. And out here, what choice did she have, anyway?

The rest of the week sped by and before she knew it, it was Thursday, time to pack her bag and go to Sarah's house.

She raced up to her room when her father brought her home from work and threw her things into her suitcase. On her way down the stairs, her mother stopped her and handed her a basket.

"Here are some cookies and a cake for you girls. Don't eat them all at once."

"Mother, as if we would. We have to watch our figures, you know. Thank you, though."

"Are you ready to go?" her father asked as he walked out of the parlor into the entryway.

"Yes, thank you for giving me a ride, Papa," Rachel said.

"After what happened at the social, I absolutely do not want you on the streets alone. Remember that," George said emphatically. "It isn't seemly for a young lady to be unescorted anyway."

"Yes, Papa," she replied meekly. She knew he was right, but how in the world would she ever get away to catch the train back east if he was watching her every move? Since the attack, he had been ever vigilant.

When they arrived at her sister's house, Sarah came out to meet them. "Will you come in, Papa?" she asked.

"No, not this time, dear. You mother and I have plans to take supper with some folks we've met at the church, tonight. Another time. You girls have a good time together." He got out and helped his younger daughter down and carried her bag into the house. He told the girls goodbye and went on his way.

Once they were alone, Sarah said, "Well, for your first night, I thought we might go to the hotel and eat at the restaurant. The food there is really good."

"All right," Rachel said. "It will be good to get out. Papa has had the eagle eye on me ever since the social. All I do is go to the library and go home."

"Well, he does have good reason, although those men are in jail. It still isn't safe to be out alone. And with Joshua gone—"

"Joshua? What does he have to do with anything?" Rachel interrupted.

"Oh, come now, little sister. I've seen the way he looks at you. Don't tell me you haven't noticed."

"And what if he does look at me a certain way? Means nothing to me."

Sarah only smiled and grabbed her shawl and reticule. "Whatever you say. Come, let's go before the restaurant gets crowded and we have to wait for a table."

They walked the few blocks to the hotel and found a table. After placing their orders for lemonade, the two sisters looked over the menu, trying to decide what sounded good to them.

When the waitress returned, Sarah said, "I think I'll have the chicken and dumplings tonight."

The woman wrote down the order and turned to Rachel. "And for you, miss?"

"Um, I'll have the roast beef special. Thank you." She handed her menu to the server.

"Now, what do you want to do for the next three days?" Sarah asked when the waitress left.

"I need to go see Annabelle to pick up the rest of the dresses she has made for me, for one thing. I haven't had the time."

"We can do that. I'm sure she'd love to have visitors. But she comes to town on Saturdays, so we should go tomorrow."

They continued to make plans for shopping, and Sarah asked if she'd like to learn to bake.

Rachel nearly spit out her lemonade. "Me? Bake?"

"Well, it wouldn't hurt you to learn how to bake one or two things. We'll start with something easy, like a cake."

"Mother sent a cake and some cookies for us."

"I know that, but it doesn't mean you can't bake one too. You can bake one for Joshua when he gets back."

"Why on earth would I do that?" Rachel asked.

"Really, Rachel, you can deny it all you want, but I know you find him attractive. What girl wouldn't?"

"A girl who has no intention of being tied down to a laborer, that's who."

Sarah started to say something but stopped herself. "I didn't know my sister was that shallow."

"What a horrible thing to say. I don't wish to argue, Sarah, but I never planned to come out west. I had no choice. That doesn't mean I have to marry a rancher or a ranch hand or a roughneck or whatever."

"I understand. I know you were not happy to leave your social circle and friends behind to come here. But you need to give the town and the men here a chance. You never know when love will find you."

"I suppose you are right about that. It's just that I have always set my sights high. I know you are happy here, but I don't think it's where I want to be for the rest of my life."

Their food arrived and they stopped talking for a bit while they ate.

Finally, Sarah said, "Well, let's not argue about it. All I'm asking is that you give it all a chance. Especially Joshua. He is a very nice young man, with a good head on his shoulders. Not bad to look at, either."

Rachel grinned at the last remark. "He is handsome, I'll have to give him that."

The time went quickly. On Friday, they visited with Annabelle. Rachel was pleased with her new wardrobe, and they stayed for tea before going back into town to do some shopping. When they got home, Sarah cooked a nice supper for the two of them and then they talked about everything under the sun. They reminisced and also talked of the future, while having cookies and milk.

Saturday was baking day, and true to her word, Sarah helped her sister bake a chocolate cake. It didn't turn out half bad for a first try. They had it for dessert that night. Sunday morning, they went to church and then to the restaurant again. Rachel enjoyed seeing some familiar faces. She had met several people by now. At the restaurant, they were joined by their parents and a few other folks.

The rest of the day was a lazy one for them. Rachel did some reading while Sarah worked on her embroidery. They turned in early. And when Monday arrived, she helped Sarah tidy the house for Conrad's return.

"This has been so much fun. We'll have to do it again sometime," Sarah said as she hugged her sister. "I'm going to start supper now. You will stay, won't you? Conrad can take you home after we eat."

"Oh, I don't want to impose. Won't you two want to be alone?"

"We will be, after supper. Now, say you'll stay. You can hear all about the trip. I'm sure Joshua will stay too."

Sarah busied herself in the kitchen after that, preparing a meal fit for a king. Well, Rachel supposed Conrad was her king in a way. She shook her head, thinking about how different she and her older sister were. She could not imagine putting one man before all else in her life, making him the center of her world. No, she much preferred to be the social butterfly. Even after the trauma of the social, she had convinced herself that she hadn't done anything wrong. Those boys were just a bad sort.

"We have half a cake left, should I bake another?" she asked Sarah.

Rachel didn't miss the smile on her sister's face. Well, let Sarah think she was turning her into a domestic. She could play the game. If the family thought she was conforming to life out here, it would make it easier for her to quietly take her leave. They wouldn't know she was gone until it was too late. Of course, her father could come after her, but she figured between Aunt Mary and herself, they could talk him into letting her stay in Philadelphia.

She set about placing all the ingredients she needed on the counter. After mixing the batter, she put it in the oven and cleaned up her mess. She was just finishing when they heard the men come in.

Rachel turned and her eyes landed on Joshua. What a handsome man he was, dressed in his Sunday clothes. Why he would prefer to work in a dirty oil field rather than a nice office still mystified her. Sarah and Conrad kissed and went into the parlor, leaving Rachel to watch the food. Joshua stepped into the kitchen and took off his hat.

"It's nice to see you again, Rachel. Did you enjoy your time with your sister?"

"I did. And you, how was your trip to the city?" she countered.

"It was busy, not much time to do anything but attend meetings, eat and sleep, actually."

"I still cannot quite comprehend why Conrad would take one of his roughnecks with him for important meetings," she said.

"Ah," he replied with a chuckle. "Since I am new, he thought it would be good experience for me. Next time, he will most likely take someone else. No big mystery."

"I see," she said, although she really didn't. But it was no concern to her except her idle curiosity.

She took her cake out of the oven to cool and checked the rest of the food, hoping her sister returned soon to finish the meal.

"Did you bake that cake yourself?" Joshua asked.

"Of course," she said simply, quite pleased with herself.

"Hmm," was all he said in response.

Before she could ask him what he meant by that remark, her sister and Conrad walked into the kitchen. Conrad had removed his jacket.

"I'll have the food on the table in a few minutes. Why don't you two go to the dining room and relax? I'm sure you are tired and hungry after your travels," Sarah said sweetly. Turning to Rachel, she asked, "Help me please?"

"Of course," Rachel said as she prepared to carry the bowls of food to the table after her sister filled them.

She carried the vegetables and Sarah followed with the meat platter. There was fresh bread and butter and lemonade to drink. Conrad said Grace and began to pass the food.

When everyone had filled their plate, he asked, "What did you ladies do to keep yourselves busy while we were away?"

The conversation during supper centered around Sarah and Rachel's exploits. Rachel excused herself to ice the cake, and surprisingly, the men both said it was good. She offered to send a few slices home with Joshua. She was proud of her accomplishment although she didn't know when her newfound skill would be needed once she got back east.

When the dishes were finished, Rachel said, "I'm going to just grab my bags and head home. I'm sure you two have things to talk about."

"I need to leave as well if I'm going to be at the site at sunup," Joshua said. "May I give you a ride home? My buggy is parked out back."

"You have a buggy?" Rachel asked, surprised.

He laughed. "Yes, I purchased one when I first came out west. You never know when it will come in handy."

A few minutes later, she brought her bags from the guest bedroom and Joshua carried them out. "I'll meet you out front," he said.

She said her goodbyes to her sister and brother-in-law, thanking her sister for inviting her to stay with her. Then she waited on the porch for Joshua to bring the buggy around.

After he helped her up into the seat beside him, he cracked the whip and they were on their way.

"I didn't know your horse was in the shed with Conrad's all these days. Sarah went out to feed theirs but didn't mention yours," she said to make conversation.

"I rode into town and left my buggy and horse at their house," he said. "So it sounds like the two of you had a nice time together."

"Yes, we did," she replied. "I have to work at the library tomorrow."

"Do you like it there?"

"It's all right, I suppose. I like the lady I work with and it's good to chat with folks when they come in."

Small talk, Rachel thought as she stole a glance at the man beside her. It was really too bad he chose not to make something of his life. She could see herself easily falling for him, but she couldn't tie herself to a man who worked in an oil field. There just was no way that was what she envisioned for herself. A roughneck, that's what he was, and apparently, that was all he aspired to, even though he could have had the world at his feet.

When they were in front of her house, he turned to her before getting out to help her with her bags. "Rachel," he began.

"Yes?" she said, her heart suddenly hammering in her chest.

Without another word, he leaned over and placed a soft kiss on her lips. "Thank you for allowing me to escort you home. And thank you for the chocolate cake. Now, let me get you to the door." He hopped down and walked around, helped her out and then grabbed her bags and walked her to the front door. He made sure the door was unlocked so she could get in, tipped his hat, and simply said, "Goodnight, my dear Rachel," leaving her speechless on her front porch.

Honestly, she would never understand this man. He teased her, spanked her, lectured her, now he'd kissed her. *Oh well, no sense dwelling on something that can never be*, she thought as she went inside. Joshua had left her bags just inside the door, so she picked them up and carried them to her room. Her parents were in the parlor, and she stopped to say goodnight to them on her way up.

"So good to have you home, dear," her mother said. "Are you going to bed so early?"

"I have to be at the library in the morning. Papa, will you be taking me?"

"Yes, I will. Have a good night, sweetheart. You can tell us all about your time with your sister at supper tomorrow night."

In her room, she unpacked and got ready for bed. She decided to wear one of her new dresses to work, so she laid it out carefully across the chair in her room. She slid between the sheets and snuggled under the quilt. Joshua was on her mind as she tried to get comfortable. He was a mystery to her. Why, oh why, didn't he want to be a businessman in his family's firm back home? Perhaps, if she got close to him, she could convince him to return to Philadelphia with her. Now, that would change things. She could court him if that happened. Yes, she definitely would be interested in that scenario. But how to convince him?

She didn't see him for several days after that. One afternoon, he came into the library and invited her to supper.

"I was in town today and thought I would see if you would accompany me to the restaurant when you finish work for the day," he said.

"Um, well, uh, yes, I suppose. My father is supposed to pick me up after work, though."

"I'll swing by the house and tell him I'll do the honors today," he said cheerily as he smiled at her.

"Um, all right, thank you."

"I will see you in a few hours then. I must go. I have errands to attend to." And he was gone.

"Is he your beau?" Mrs. Richards whispered as she came up behind her. "I must say he is very good looking."

Rachel could feel the blush rising on her cheeks as she replied, "Just a friend. He invited me to supper after work."

"I'd say that young man has more in mind than being your friend. A nice young lady such as yourself would do well with a man like that one, I dare say."

"Well, I-I should get back to work now," Rachel said as she busied herself cataloguing the new books that had come in.

A few hours later, she found herself sitting in the local restaurant with Joshua. He had picked her up and now they were sipping tea as they waited for their meal to arrive. They were chatting amicably until he leaned across the table and took her hand in his.

"Rachel, there is something I want to ask you. It's the reason I invited you to join me this evening."

She looked into his eyes. What was he about to ask?

"We have known each other since the train. And we have been together on several occasions since then. I think the next step is for me to start officially courting you."

No, no, no! Why? she thought to herself. A part of her wanted to say 'yes, of course, please, yes.' But that other part, the part that had been leading her until now warned her it could never be.

"Rachel?" he asked. "Surely, this is no surprise to you."

"I-I, well, Joshua, I enjoy your company, but I think you want different things than I do. Let me ask you a question."

"Ask me anything."

"Would you ever consider going back home to the east?"

"Rachel, I made my decision a few years ago. This is my home now. I have no desire to go back or to work in the confines of my family's firm. I am making a new life for myself. This is also your home now, might I remind you."

"No, no, it isn't. You see, that is where we differ. I plan to go back home eventually. It was not my choice to come here with my parents."

"Miss Linton!"

What was that tone he was using with her? It was stern, so stern that it made her clench her bottom cheeks, reminding her of the day of the social when he had the audacity to spank her.

"Yes, Mr. Thomas?" she asked.

"If we were not in a public place, you would be over my knee about now. Your parents brought you here so you could make a good life for yourself. They were not happy with some of your antics in Philadelphia. You have made friends, you have found meaningful work, and you are settling in. Why on earth would you even think you might go back? There is nothing there for you. Your entire family is here."

"For one thing, no, my entire family is not here. I have an aunt back home who would gladly take me in. And second, where did you get the preposterous idea that my parents moved out here for me? They came here to be near my sister. And third, you will not be placing me over your knee ever again."

She started to rise, but he stopped her, saying quietly, "I know because your father told me. Now sit down and do not make a scene, or I can promise that you will be over my knee before the night is over."

Rachel was seething by this time, but the waitress brought their food so she hid it and was polite to the woman, while ignoring her supper companion. After they had been eating for a while, she finally calmed enough to say, "I do not believe you. My father would never have told you such a thing."

"I suggest you ask him if you do not wish to take my word for it. Now, about courting you—"

She cut him off abruptly, "No. I'm sorry, but if you are not open to bettering yourself and going back east, then I am not open to allowing you to court me. I cannot be with a man who is content to work as a *roughneck* for the rest of his life."

"So be it. I had not pegged you as a shallow, selfish girl. Flighty, perhaps, but I, like your father, believed that would change once you settled in here. Finish your supper, and I will escort you home. You will not have to suffer my *roughneck* company again."

What had she just done? She had surely ruined any chance she might have had with the handsome man seated across from her. Yes, she would have had to change his mind about some things—many things—but she had been confident she could succeed in doing that. Apparently, she had been wrong. He was bullheaded and stubborn! Well, she knew what she must do now. She must devise the plan she needed to go to Aunt Mary, sooner, rather than later.

When he took her home, Joshua walked her to the door, said goodnight, and left.

She went straight to her room. Luckily, her parents were not at home, so she did not have to answer their questions about her evening. She sat in the window seat in her bedroom and formulated her escape plan. There was nothing for her here. First thing in the morning, she would send a wire to Aunt Mary, telling her she was on her way and asking her not to say anything to anyone.

Joshua Thomas could have his wild west oilfield job. She would find a more suitable man in Philadelphia, where she belonged.

Then why did she cry herself to sleep?

CHAPTER 10

AMY

*E*ver since she saw Glen and Naomi together at the social her chest tightened to the point that she feared it might disintegrate. Could her bones crumble from the pressure? It pained her to breathe. It pained her to speak. It wouldn't relent.

Immediately after realizing the loving couple strolling in front of her were Glen and Naomi, she circled and darted away. Stopping when it became impossible to inhale any air and an unbearable pain debilitated her.

Hunched over and gasping for breath, Jose came upon her. He lowered himself to one knee and stroked her back. "What is it? Are you unwell?" he asked. His concern evident in his tone and touch.

She shouldn't have come. Such a bad idea. Did she possess the ability to make any good choices anymore? She broke Lola's rules by leaving the Parlor. She rejected and defied Glen's advice on the matter. She encountered a desperate Lizzie and agreed to assist further in eliminating her pregnancy. And... she observed her husband with another woman. And at the very event he declined attending with her.

Everything seemed hopeless. Once she met with Lizzie and did as she promised, she planned to confront Glen and return home. She hated it there. She hated him. How could he be so cruel?

Jose pressed, an urgency in his voice, "Amy, speak to me. Tell me what it is."

Finally, she gasped and drew air into her hurting lungs. Straightening, she breathed deep and slow. She caught sight of a man up ahead waving his arm at her. Mr. O'Brien. She couldn't tackle another thing. Snatching Jose's hand, she pleaded, "I am feeling ill. Please escort me home." *Home.* She had a home. Back east.

She managed to direct Jose out of Mr. O'Brien's path. He grasped her hand and didn't release it. They walked in silence, but he kept the pace slow and glanced at her often. "We should take you to the doctor. You said you were unwell last evening. And now again," Jose urged.

"I wish to lie down. I'm fatigued. Once I rest, I am sure I will be good as new," she insisted.

Thankfully, Jose didn't pursue it. "I hope that is true. I will not call on you tonight. But I have a request."

Halting, she gazed at him dreading his request. She doubted she could ever deny him anything, but she lacked the strength to comply with any additional appeal. She deflected, "I apologize. I know you paid for a consecutive week at the Parlor. Your last paid visit is tomorrow. If we miss tonight, Lola will not grant you an additional night."

A reassuring grin complemented the kindness in his gaze. "I request you tell your employer you can't entertain this evening. Not because I won't be present, though that is a viable excuse, but because you are unwell and need to rest."

Because he won't be present offers a viable excuse? Had Jose adopted a role of guardian for her? Her insides warmed and flut-tered at the idea. Though he usually arrived after her customers left and at an hour late enough Lola wouldn't allow newcomers, she now wondered if he did so with intention. Intention other than him conceding to the shallowness of others forcing shame on his heritage. Could he do it because he cared enough to verify that she went to bed alone, safe and comfortable each night? The opposite of her husband. She and Jose would never be. She decided against annulling her marriage. She chose to challenge Glen for an explanation. Probably receive nothing in return. No explanation. No apology. And return home.

She would never marry a man who loved and adored her. She would never have children. She would die alone never having experienced fully sharing herself with a man. The man she loved. The man whose tender touches and obvious attrac-tion sparked in her a mutual desire. Jose.

"I promise," she replied. As if she could attend the evening's affairs. She wanted to crawl into her bed and cry. Cry until her eyes dried up and became as brittle as the bones in her chest felt.

They chuckled as they both sighed stopping at the steps to the Parlor. Jose watched her with his embracing brown eyes. Without touching one another, she imagined him hugging her tightly and vowing all would be okay.

Bending closer, he pressed his lips to her forehead. "I will see you tomorrow. If I find you in the same state, we will pay the doctor a visit."

She nodded and bolted for the door. If she didn't, she worried she never would. Her heart ached because she must leave Jose behind. Not Glen.

Luckily, she retained enough wits to realize she couldn't rush inside. Per the house rules, she should never have left. Without witnessing it with her eyes, she knew Jose stood where she left him. As he probably would until she went inside.

Thinking quickly, she concocted another lie. She truly had

become a liar. "I forgot… I have some clothes on the line drying. I will go take them down and go in the back," she stated.

Stepping back, Jose smiled and watched as she hurried to the back to do as she claimed. Picking up a few pebbles, she threw them at Josie's window. Missing multiple times. Finally, she struck her target. Josie's face peered through the window before vanishing.

The kitchen door opened, and Josie waved her over. Throwing a nightdress over Amy's shoulders concealing her common dress, Josie rambled in a whisper. "Hurry. Hurry. It has been as if someone lit a stick of dynamite in here today. I hope to goodness you weren't involved in any of the detonation."

Not something else to contend with. Naomi. Had Naomi seen her? Did she start trouble again for and about her? Amy could burn her too. And between the shock and despair of the day, a fury blazed. Amy would depart them all with her voice being heard. No longer would she fold to theirs or anyone's demands. She would leave on her terms. With her head held high. They couldn't break her.

They made it through the kitchen and upstairs without notice. Josie pulled her inside the room and closed the door quietly. "What is wrong with you? Have you not heard a word I said?" Josie asked in a panicked flurry of arms and facial expressions.

Amy shrugged. She didn't care. How sad. She honestly no longer cared what occurred or didn't inside the walls of the Parlor. Except… Lizzie still required her help. "I am not accountable for whatever set off Lola this time."

Josie smirked and sat on the bed. "So… you weren't present when that snooty li'l twit propositioned a couple of the Beecher brothers then denied it and had them arrested?" She slapped her hands on the top of her thighs and grimaced. "I've had my eye on Joshua Thomas forever. Any time I see him in town I ask him to come see me. So, not only have I lost him to the prissy leech, but I've also lost two of the Beecher brothers until they are released."

None of what Josie bemoaned about applied to Amy. Good. But, *Beecher brothers*? They didn't have any Beechers as customers. Amy yearned to get in her bed. "I don't know any Joshua Thomas. Or any prissy lady. And certainly, no Beecher brothers. You castigate me for my choices, but are you keeping company with non-paying men?"

Shrugging again, Josie stated, "We all do what we must. And those Beecher boys are well worth it. Be it their generous anatomy or their overzealous vigor. No regrets, my friend."

"It didn't involve me. I returned early. My monthly came and bad. There isn't any way I can go downstairs tonight." She prayed Josie didn't debate with her.

She did not. "I will tell Lola. On top of my insignificant issues today, seems Naomi left without permission today. That will certainly occupy Lola's attention." Pulling down the quilt, she patted the pillow. "Lie down. You don't look so well. No one will notice your absence tonight. Without my favorite two brothers, it's freed up some time for me. And you have no regular tonight." Her mouth opened with apparent additional comment, but she refrained.

"Jose won't be coming tonight," Amy declared. She offered no further information on the subject. As if Josie didn't know she spent the day with Jose. At least a few hours. And he didn't behave as a usual patron. If she were sick, he wouldn't and didn't expect her to entertain him. Perhaps Mr. O'Brien and Mr. Ramsey wouldn't either. But Glen would.

Josie's fingers kneaded the quilt. She averted her eyes and mumbled. "I am sorry. First, for forgetting him as a usual. Secondly, because he won't be coming. I suppose it didn't go as expected today. I admit I never expected it to end between the two of you. He appeared quite smitten."

It crossed her mind not to elaborate and spare Josie further disappointment, but she cared about her friend and wished she would respect herself more and not allow others to mistreat her. Witnessing the treatment that she received from her customers and now learning she enjoyed giving herself freely to a group of obviously questionable brothers substantiated what she failed to realize. She wouldn't leave without Josie. She couldn't. Josie didn't belong at the Parlor. She deserved an opportunity to find a man who treated her with kindness and lavished her in unconditional affection. Not today. Tomorrow she would discuss her plans with Josie.

"It went great. He knows I am ill and insisted I rest tonight," Amy responded.

As anticipated, Josie's brows furrowed. She frowned and her shoulders slumped. "Though he has already paid... he agreed to forfeit his fee and let you rest?" she questioned. "He put your needs above his own," she stated, but her quivering lip and watering eyes betrayed her and exhibited her disbelief.

Taking a seat beside her on the bed, Amy emphasized, "Yes. No man... whether he pays or not should ever demean you or demand you provide him something you don't want to."

Josie's head bounced in unison with her rocking torso. "I see. I mean, I hear you." She placed her hand on Amy's knee and squeezed it. "Get undressed and in bed. I'll talk to you tomorrow."

"Josie, don't leave upset. Please," Amy begged. She would see to it that the petite, kind woman who went above and beyond to please everyone around her received a life worthy of her.

Stiffening her back and jutting out her chin which bounced the red ringlets around her pretty face, Josie insisted, "I am not upset. I am happy for you. If you'll lose that fraud of a husband, perhaps you and Jose can be happy together."

Amy's chest constricted. Glen. Lizzie had been right in her assumptions. Now, Josie concurred. Tuesday morning, Glen would be out of her life. For good.

MONDAY, Amy stayed in her bed until the hour came for her to appear downstairs. It shocked her to find Jose waiting on her. He immediately led her to a sofa and had her sit. "How are you today? Better I hope," he inquired.

Discovering he showed early, earlier than any other patron, and evidently out of concern for her instantly improved her physical and mental status. She smiled at him. Her heart raced and rejoiced in his presence. This could be their last encounter. Ever. "I am better. Much better. You are here in time to take a meal with me. Would you?" she asked. She wouldn't squander the time they had left. She planned to enjoy him for as long as she could. Who knew? Maybe he had terrible table manners and it would be so off-putting that it ruined him for her forever.

No such luck. He behaved as the 'perfect gentleman'. More than any other male companion she ever dined with. He pulled out her chair. He filled her cup. He insisted she be served before him. And the conversation never ceased. It never became incessant. She cherished every story he told of his large, loving family. He urged her to speak often, but she declined. His retellings were more interesting and heartwarming than hers.

After the meal, they joined the others in the parlor room. The atmosphere was relaxed and rather silent. Josie's companion mentioned Naomi's absence. He then suggested she sing along with him while he played the piano. The mere reference to Naomi caused a surge of panic coursing through her.

Jose encouraged her to sing. The other gentleman sat on the bench behind the keys and convinced her to entertain them with his overabundance of compliments on her ability.

The song he chose centered around a couple in love who could never be together. It amazed her how autobiographical the lyrics were. And how she found liberation and an ironic healing in verbalizing her inner turmoil. She encompassed the emotions in the words and delivered them in a heartfelt performance.

Josie applauded and hugged her. She whispered, "Sorry for not seeing you today. I had a few things to take care of. Do you still have need of the female physician in the morning? He arrives at seven, in the stable, but must tend to Lola's girls first. Wait a bit and be aware. Lola can't know. The woman must pay forty dollars."

Amy returned the hug forcibly enough to transmit her appreciation. "Yes. Thank you."

After a few more songs, Jose advised her he must go. He worked that day, tended the crops, and had another long day tomorrow. He raised his face and went to kiss her forehead. She too lifted her face.

Their lips connected. As she orchestrated.

They stilled. She had her eyes open and watched his widen. Their eyes met. One of his arms looped around her side pulling her closer to him. The other rose and his fingers caressed her face. Softly and slowly, he kissed her. His lips moved over hers. They would stall and linger and savor before resuming their easy exploration. They were never intrusive. Never beckoning. They were hypnotic. It was as if he wanted to taste and touch every inch of them. But without any other goal or expectation besides that.

She craved more. Being around Jose deferred her demons and gave her hope of how things could be but touching him torched them and generated a fire in her.

A loud clearing of someone's throat had them reluctantly break their kiss and step away from one another. They both turned and saw Virgil. He arched an eyebrow and grumbled, "Miss Amy does not take guests upstairs."

Jose stammered, "No... no, of course not. I meant no disrespect." Reaching for the doorknob, he nodded at her. "If I can manage it, I will return tomorrow and hopefully retain our nightly visits."

The impulse to throw her arms around him and beg him to take her with him overwhelmed her. At least she should confide in him and advise him not to bother as she wouldn't be there.

She did neither.

Be it her regret over not doing either, or all the other stressful situations, she tossed and turned all night. And it showed when she washed and dressed the next morning. Her eyes were puffy from lack of sleep and all the crying. Her coloring appeared dull.

Sneaking out of the Parlor and to the hotel, she glimpsed Lizzie pacing. She thought she looked terrible, but Lizzie looked worse.

Rushing to greet and comfort her friend, Amy stated, "I didn't realize it was necessary we wait before going. Let's go inside and have a cup of coffee in the restaurant."

Lizzie's big, blue eyes were sad and scared. "I brought money. I didn't know how much, but I believe I have enough," she quavered.

Leading her inside, Amy offered, "If you don't, I have it. I will be with you through the entire thing. I won't leave you. I promise."

Miss Wilson noticed them before they decided on a table and shuffled over. "Two beautiful faces on such a glorious morning brightens my day. I hope you've given some thought into taking a shift over the weekends. It just isn't the same without you."

"Good morning, Mrs. Wilson. Honestly, I have, but things keep popping up demanding my attention. I promise to get with you soon. We both will have a cup of coffee," Amy replied.

"Great. Great. I have fresh biscuits and gravy this morning if either of you get a hankering." Mrs. Wilson bustled away leaving the two women to themselves.

Amy didn't know what to say. Or not say. Lizzie's eyes were

wide, and she continuously twitched. It's not as if either of them desired making small talk. Amy had arranged and Lizzie intended to participate in an immoral and illegal procedure.

Almost an hour went by without a word, and Lizzie's shaking worsened. She could barely lift her cup to her mouth. It clanked into her teeth and onto the saucer when she lowered it. "I can't do it," she declared. "I won't." Tears welled in her eyes, and she darted out of her seat and from the restaurant.

Paying their bill, Amy found her outside hunched over between two buildings vomiting. "Oh, Lizzie. You don't have to. No one can force you to." Fetching a handkerchief from her purse, the one she forgot about, the one with the initials N. C., she held it out to Lizzie.

Taking the handkerchief and wiping her mouth, a changed Lizzie raised and met her. Her eyes were bright and determined. Her shoulders square and purposeful. "It is my baby. I hope Floyd will accept it as his own. The conception as ugly and offensive as it was... is of no fault of my own. Nor Floyd's. And certainly not the child's."

Amy took her hands. "Floyd will not disappoint you. He is a wonderful man, and he loves you greatly."

"Let us go and pay the physician for his time. It is imperative I go to my husband." Throwing her arms around Amy's shoulders, she hugged her tightly. "You have gone above and beyond. I will never forget it."

They strolled along, arm in arm. Judging by Lizzie's chatter and her excitement, she acknowledged the baby as the miracle she should. Hopefully, she could heal from the trauma Howard Slater inflicted. Amy believed she would.

Turning onto the back, disreputable road, the rambling about having a baby and wonderings over if it could be a girl or boy ended. The realization of where they were and where they were going gained her focus. Lizzie cautioned, "We should not be here. Oh no. All this time I've been preoccupied with my troubles, I never inquired about yours."

Clutching her regretful friend's arm to her bosom, Amy asserted, "Do not apologize to me. I am fine. We will handle this transaction, and you will be on your way to share your news with Floyd."

"I do believe he and I are strong as a couple. He, as I, will concentrate on the blessing God bestowed upon us." Dropping her hand to her abdomen, she rubbed it lovingly. "I'm having a baby," she gushed.

Approaching the Parlor, a commotion of raised voices and threats were heard. Amy prayed they weren't coming from the Parlor. Stopping at the side of the building before heading toward the back, she viewed the scene.

Glen, Floyd, and Lola were arguing in front of the stable. Pivoting to lead Lizzie away without notice failed.

Glen charged them. "What in hell are you planning to do? You arranged for the termination of Lizzie's pregnancy? Of my niece or nephew?" he badgered.

Floyd rushed to Lizzie and stopped short. He gazed at her with such love and confusion and disappointment, she empathized with him, and tears sprang from her eyes.

"Lizzie... no. Tell me you wouldn't do such a thing. Please—" Floyd pleaded.

Going to him, Lizzie placed her palms on his face. "I thought I had to, but I decided not to. It's not your child."

He closed his eyes and nodded. "I know. I don't care. Anything that is a part of you I must be a part of. I can't imagine it any other way. I don't wish to live any other way."

Planting her lips on his, they shared a desperate and consoling kiss. "Never," she mumbled a barely audible acquiescence.

A positive or a negative, Naomi marched into the confrontation. "Well, Nathan, is this enough to finally incite you to stop lollygagging around and proceed with your supposed reprisal?" she demanded.

Nathan. Reprisal. "What is she speaking of? I saw the two of you. Together. At the social. I'm your wife. Why?" Amy implored.

"No. You aren't my wife. I paid a drunk to pretend to marry us. We had no witnesses. Naomi is my wife. It went too far. I never meant to deceive you. At least for not as long as I have. I got deeper and deeper until I couldn't foresee any easy solution."

"Solution. You're a selfish, ignorant man, Nathan Chumley!" Naomi yelled. She stomped up to him and slapped him across his face. The smack echoed in the otherwise quiet alley.

Nathan Chumley. The initials on the handkerchief. "What happened to Glen? You must have met him. You had my picture." Why would he pretend to be Glen? Why would he force her to believe they were married?

Snatching Naomi's wrist, Glen glared at her. "I reckon I can't delay the inevitable any longer."

As if heaven answered a prayer she had yet to recognize, Jose grabbed her from behind and flung her beside him. "Don't you touch her. Don't even think of it. You are a manipulative bastard," he accused.

Glen hung his head. "Yes. Yes, I am. But as cunning as I am, I never dishonored Amy. Irving Slater, Howard's father and the grandfather to Lizzie's baby is to arrive at the Big G today. He and his wife, Laura Garrison's mother, are there to visit. Today is not the day I predicted everything would be revealed and hopefully concluded. But Naomi is correct. I've delayed far too long." He tugged Naomi along behind him. "Everyone, head to the Big G."

Lola's hard tone and menacing words interrupted their departure. "Not a one of you is welcome back here. Naomi gathered her things yesterday, but I recommend you do the same... now, Amy. You won't gain admittance again."

CHAPTER 11

RACHEL

*R*achel woke with a pounding headache after crying for most of the night. She had slept fitfully when she had finally nodded off. She forced herself to get up, padding over to the basin in her room. She splashed her face, threw on her robe and went to the kitchen.

"Rachel, aren't you feeling well, dear? You look like you may be coming down with something," her mother said when she saw her.

"I have a case of the sniffles is all. I thought maybe a cup of tea would help."

"Why don't you go on back up to bed since you aren't expected at the library today? I'll bring you up some tea and toast."

"Thank you, Mama," she said as she turned to head back upstairs.

"How was your supper with Joshua last night?" her mother asked before she got out of the room.

"It was fine. We came to an agreement that we are just not right for each other," she said and hurriedly ran out of the room.

When her mother came up a little later with her tea and toast, she sat down on the edge of the bed and rubbed Rachel's forehead. "I think maybe the sniffles you've come down with may have something to do with what you told me earlier. Whose decision was that, darling?"

"I do not wish to talk about it. As I said, we both agreed. That is all there is to it."

"All right, dear. I won't press you. Try to rest today. I'll make you some soup for lunch. Maybe you'll feel better by then."

Rachel watched her mother leave the room and quietly shut the door. Taking a few bites of the toast, she pushed the plate aside, unable to eat any more. She sipped the hot, sweet tea and wiped a stray tear that had found its way to her cheek. *I won't cry over him! I won't.*

She finished the tea and set the tray on her bedside table. Then she went back to sleep for a few hours. When she woke again, she reached into a drawer and got paper and pen out to write a letter to her aunt. She'd decided against sending a wire. Posting a letter would be better. No one would know she had sent it. She could take it to the post on her break tomorrow when she was at the library. By the time her aunt received it, she would be on her way.

When that was finished, she hid the letter in her drawer and got up to bathe. She went into the water closet and when she was finished, she dressed and went downstairs.

"Oh, I was just going to bring up some soup. You look like you are feeling much better," her mother said.

"I am, thank you. Why don't you sit and have some soup with me?" Rachel offered.

"I think I will do that. Your father is having lunch with some of his new friends today."

Rachel tried to keep the conversation off herself, so she asked, "How is the quilting coming along?"

"Oh, I'm enjoying it immensely. The ladies at the church are so nice and helpful."

The conversation continued and Rachel only half listened as her mother talked about all her new friends. Why was it that both her parents seemed to really like living here?

There was a knock on the door and then Sarah breezed in. "Hello, you two. I just stopped by to let you know I'll be staying with Kate for a few days out at the farm. The doctor has ordered her to bed, and Conrad and I thought I should go help out until she is feeling better."

"Is it the baby?" her mother asked.

"The baby is fine. Kate just caught a bug of some sort and the doctor wants her to get plenty of rest."

"Is there anything I can do to help? I know, take some of this soup to her. I'll make some other food and your father and I will bring it out to the farm later."

"Oh, Mother, that would be wonderful. Thank you. I'm sure Kate and Jim will appreciate that."

"And I'll make sure Conrad is fed as well. Tell him he can come here for supper each night while you are out at the farm."

"I will pass that along to him. I really must go now. He is taking a break from work to run me out there, so I don't want to keep him waiting. I'll see you later. Rachel, nice to see you. We'll catch up another time." Sarah took the soup her mother handed her and was out the door.

Rachel nodded and got up to fix her mother and herself some more tea.

"I guess I should get started cooking," her mother said as she got up too.

"I can bake a cake for them," Rachel offered, ignoring the look of surprise on her mother's face.

"You want to bake a cake? I don't, um, really have time to help you if I'm going to get some meals together for them, dear."

"Don't worry. I can bake a chocolate cake. Sarah and I baked when I stayed with her."

"Well, all right. That would be nice. I will get some meat cooking."

The two of them worked side by side for the next few hours. Mrs. Linton fixed vegetables, a roast and baked a couple of pies. Rachel's cake turned out nicely, and by the time her father returned to the house and her mother explained the situation, he said he would take her and the food out to the farm.

"I'd like to ride along if it's all right," Rachel said.

Both parents turned to look at her as if she'd suddenly grown two heads. Finally, her mother said, "Of course, dear. Get ready, and we'll leave in just a few minutes."

Rachel ran up to her room to tidy her hair. She did want to see Kate one more time before she left, so now was as good a time as any. She hated it that she wouldn't be here to see the baby after he or she was born, but it just wasn't meant to be. She would be back east by then, reestablishing her place in society.

When she came downstairs, her father was putting the food in the buggy and her mother was waiting for her in the foyer. "Let's go, dear, so they can have this meal for supper tonight."

When they arrived at the farm, Sarah had things under control. She was doing the washing, and Kate was sleeping.

"She had some soup and then nodded off," Sarah told them as she took the food from her father. "Thank you, Mother. We'll eat this tonight. The ranch hands will fend for themselves for now. They have a few who are capable of cooking a simple meal. I've already spoken to them and promised to cook one big meal for all of them before I go back home. I'll just have to look after Kate and Jim and the household chores until she is back on her feet."

"How is she doing?" her mother asked.

"She just needs to rest. She said she is feeling much better.

The doctor will look in on her in a few days. I'm sure she'll be back up and around after that."

"Sarah?" a voice called out from the bedroom.

"Sounds like our patient is awake. I'll be right back and we can have some tea before you go."

When Sarah returned, she said that Kate was awake and if they wanted to go in and visit with her while she made tea, they could.

"Why don't you and Rachel go? I'll stay out here and keep Sarah company, see if she needs anything before we leave," Mr. Linton said.

Rachel was glad to see Kate sitting up in bed.

"Come in. I'm so happy to see both of you. Sarah said you made a meal for us. That was so thoughtful. I don't know what I would do without dear Sarah. She dropped everything to come out as soon as she heard I was under the weather."

"It was the least we could do. Rachel even baked a cake."

"Really? How sweet of you, dear. How are you settling in by now? I know the move has been difficult for you."

Rachel replied, "I am working a couple of days a week at the library, and I have met a few folks."

"Oh, that's wonderful. I knew it wouldn't take long for you to feel at home," Kate said with a smile.

Rachel felt just a tiny bit of remorse that she was deceiving Sarah's sweet sister-in-law, but she couldn't let anyone suspect what she was planning.

Sarah brought in the tea and they had a nice visit before it was time to go.

"We don't want to tire you out. You get better soon," Mrs. Linton said as she stood to leave.

When they got back to town, George suggested they go to the restaurant for supper so his wife wouldn't have to cook another meal. Rachel went along, hoping she didn't run into Joshua since she knew he frequented the place often. Luckily, he was not there. After supper, they went home and she excused herself to go to her room. She had a lot to do.

After packing and shoving her bags under the bed, she went over her plan again. Everything was set. Tomorrow, she would post the letter to her aunt, and in just a few days, she would be on her way. She just had to figure out how to get to the train station without being seen.

~

JOSHUA

"Easy there, Josh. Safety first," Clyde, the driller and Annabelle's husband, said as he noticed Josh handling some of the equipment roughly. "What's eatin' you today, son?"

"Nothing."

"Now, I've been around long enough to know it's something. Wanna talk about it? I am a good listener, you know."

"Well, let's take a break, then," Joshua said as he took off his hat and wiped the sweat from his brow.

"Sounds good to me. The boys can handle things for a few minutes," Clyde said. He turned to the crew and told one of his other roughnecks he and Josh were taking a short break. "Handle things until I get back."

The two men walked to where there was some shade and Clyde poured coffee for both of them, handing one mug to the younger man. "Now, tell me what's got you so all fired mad today. Or can I take a wild guess that it has something to do with Conrad's pretty little sister-in-law?"

"You guessed right. You don't know how much I wanted to turn that sassy little girl over my knee last night at supper and blister her bottom so she wouldn't sit for a damn week!"

"Why didn't you find a place to do it when you left? We've all been in that predicament, son. Tell me what she did that got you so riled up."

"I mentioned that since we had known each other since the train ride out here and had gone out a few times together, seen each other at family dinners and such, it might be time for me to start officially courting her. I already have George's approval."

"And she didn't cotton to the idea, I take it," Clyde said thoughtfully as he sipped his hot coffee.

"I'm not good enough for her is more like it. What a snob-bish, cheeky little—"

"Whoa, don't say something you'll regret, boy. What exactly did she say?"

"Oh, that we don't want the same things out of life. Basically, I have no ambition because I've made my home here and choose to do manual labor rather than sit in my father's office all day back home. She says this will never be her home and she is going back to Philadelphia someday. Asked if I would go."

"And you said no," Clyde supplied.

"Damn right I did."

"Josh, this may not be any of my business, but why don't you just tell her the truth?"

The younger man looked at him and said, "If you think that I would do that now, you're crazy, Clyde. If she can't accept me for who she thinks I am, then I sure as hell am not going to accept her when she finds out different."

"I guess I can see your point there. You want her to love you no matter what kind of work you do. Makes sense."

"You see, I didn't want her to know the truth, not until I was sure I had won her heart. I want her to love me for myself, not for my money or social standing. I chose not to stay back east. I made the decision to stay here when I inherited all that money from my grandfather. I get enough grief about that from my family, I sure as hell don't need it from the woman I love."

"Do you love her?" Clyde asked.

Joshua hesitated and then said, "I have loved her since we became acquainted on the train, I believe. I hoped to make her fall in love with Joshua Thomas, roughneck, before I told her the truth. You see, Rachel has absurd ideas about social standing and the kind of man she can marry. I don't fit into her plans as a ranch hand or a roughneck."

"Damn, it's a hard call to make. If she knew the truth, she would probably change her mind. On the other hand, you'd always wonder if she loved you for *you*."

"Exactly. Please do not mention this to Conrad. I don't wish for her family to know. They have such high hopes for her to settle in and fall in love with this town and its people. I just don't think that is going to happen."

"If she is planning to go back east, shouldn't someone warn them?"

"I didn't get the impression she meant soon."

"Then you have time to work on winning her heart."

"Nope. Not gonna try. She made her feelings perfectly clear."

"I still say you should have blistered her bottom."

Joshua laughed. "We need to get back to work."

When his shift was over, Joshua made his way back to the bunkhouse at the Big G. He had hoped to be moved into his own place soon, but now, he decided to wait just a little longer. What was the point?

He washed up and then ate a simple meal of beans and left-over cornbread Mrs. Garrison had baked the night before and sent to him. After that, he went to his bunk and crawled in, exhausted, and tried to fall asleep. But images of a little wisp of a feisty girl across his lap made him hard and since no one was in the bunkhouse this early, he relieved himself before trying to sleep again. Damn that woman! How had he let her get under his skin?

Maybe Clyde was right. Maybe he should have tried to spank

some sense into her. Well, it was too late now. He had his pride, after all.

He finally slept, and for the next few days, he went about his usual routine. He worked at the site, met with Conrad to go over things in the office, and made sure Mr. Ryan was doing all right and had everything he needed. Should he have told Rachel the truth that only Clyde, Sarah and Conrad knew about him? No! Damn it. She should have fallen in love with him, not his position in life. And since she was not willing to give that a chance, so be it. He had always been stubborn and he guessed some things never changed, because he'd be damned if he told her now.

One evening, he walked into the restaurant and saw Rachel with her sister. He turned around and walked right back out, going to the general store and picking up sandwich fixings for his supper instead. Another time, he saw her walking down the street and turned to go the other way. He was avoiding her, and he hoped she noticed.

At the office, Conrad tried to talk to him about it, but he told him it was over and done with and there was nothing more to say. "She made her decision."

Conrad only shook his head, but he didn't press him.

He bought a bottle of whiskey on his day off and drank himself into oblivion. Then he slept it off and drank a pot of coffee before heading to the site the next morning. He hadn't shaved in days, and frankly, he didn't care. If Rachel thought of him as a heathen, then he would be one.

That was the day they struck oil at the Big G. The crew had been working around the clock, taking shifts, waiting for it to happen. Clyde had begun to think they had been wrong and they weren't going to strike, but five thousand feet in and it happened. The crew began dancing around the derrick, celebrating. Clyde and Joshua exchanged a look of relief, and Joshua left to tell Conrad the news while the roughnecks began the next phase of running pipe in the well.

He got on his horse and raced into town. He found Conrad sitting behind his desk working on some contracts when he burst in, excited as hell. "We hit at the Big G!"

"Well, thank God," Conrad said with a sigh of relief. "Sit down, Josh, let's have a drink to celebrate."

He took a bottle from his desk drawer and poured a shot for both of them. When he handed one to Josh, he held his own up to toast, "To the start of our joint venture! May this only be the beginning."

"Here, here," Joshua said and then drank his down.

Conrad poured them both another. "I can't wait to tell Sarah. You need to tell Rachel."

Joshua looked at him and said, "Now, why would I do that?"

Conrad sighed and said, "Do you love that girl?"

"You know how I feel."

"You need to do something about it, man. Or you are going to lose her for good."

"I've already lost her, partner."

"Have you?"

"I should get back to the site. We'll talk later. You get on home and tell your beautiful wife the good news."

All the way back, he thought about what Conrad had said. It would be nice to have someone waiting at home to hear the good news. Conrad was a very lucky man. But he wasn't going to spill his guts to Rachel now. Not after she had made her true feelings known to him. He had seen a side to her he didn't like. Sure, he'd known what her dad had said about her and he'd seen some of it for himself, but he didn't think she would actually tell him that he wasn't good enough for her. If she knew the truth, she would try to make up to him, and that, he couldn't stomach.

And what if he had turned her over his lap that night? Would it have changed anything?

When he got back to the drilling site, the men were still busy running pipe and doing the necessary things. Clyde was supervising, and soon, the next shift would be coming on duty.

"Well, how'd Conrad take the news?" Clyde asked when Joshua got off his horse and tied him to a tree.

"He was relieved, I think. We celebrated with a drink and he was off to tell Sarah the good news."

"Good, good. Why don't you join us for a celebration? The next shift will be coming on soon, and these guys have all earned a good meal and a stiff drink. I've invited them all over to my place after they get cleaned up."

"What will your wife say about that?" Joshua teased.

"I sent word to her. My Annabelle will have no problem with it. And there are all the cousins around to help her get a feast prepared on short notice. That's how our family is."

"All right then. I'll head to the bunkhouse and get cleaned up, then meet you there."

"When you gonna move into your house? I think it's about time you took your rightful spot now, don't you?"

Joshua just shook his head and told his driller he would see him soon.

As he got ready for the celebration, he asked himself the same question. Was it time to move on and take up residence in his own home? And should he let his real position with Appleby Oil be known? Conrad had wanted to add his name to the company since he'd invested, but Joshua had declined. He didn't need his name on the office door. He was learning the business from the ground up.

When he got to the Gonzales' place, things were in full swing. Clyde's family had set up tables in the yard and there was food and drink aplenty. Everyone was happy, music was playing, and folks were dancing and talking.

He enjoyed the festivities, but in the back of his mind, he thought how nice it would be if Rachel was there with him.

CHAPTER 12

AMY

No one followed Glen. It escaped his notice until he sat on his horse and positioned Naomi in front of him. "What are you all waiting for? I owe you all answers, a lot of them, and I don't deserve it, but I pray I one day receive your forgiveness." He forcibly swallowed, a motion visible to all, and dipped his head before situating his hat. "It is necessary we all go to the Big G. Confessing my transgressions is shameful enough without having to do it multiple times. Please come and listen."

Floyd's attention went to Lizzie. Not that it ever left her. He cupped her chin, lifted her face, and addressed her devotedly. "He says Irving Slater will be there. I know he is mortified by Howard's actions. It is your decision. We do not have to expose either of you to anything you aren't comfortable with. If you choose to not involve anyone but us in our child's life... I support you."

Placing one hand on her abdomen, the other she brought to Floyd's head and fiddled with his long, wispy strands, Lizzie agreed, "This is our child. But he or she should receive the love of all its relatives in addition to ours. I have no reason to deny Irving Slater the opportunity to know his grandchild. No matter the sins of his son and the baby's father."

A horse's hooves stamping in the dirt and the familiar defiant shake of its head reiterated the need to react. Naomi elbowed Glen in the ribs as the horse bucked and reared to go. "I hate it when you force me to ride with you. I'm able to manage my own horse," she seethed.

"This came about suddenly. Not like I could acquire a wagon... or carriage, or a horse of your own," Glen defended.

All these weeks Glen forbade Amy from interacting with anyone from the Big G. Now he urged her to go there. Her head pounded. The pressure in her eyes thumped with her rapid heart rate. Squinting, she barely noticed Floyd and Lizzie leave the alley. Jose questioned, "What do you wish to do, Amy? We need to go and gather your things. I can put you up with my aunts until you... until you figure out where and what will make you happiest."

Happiest. She would settle for happy. Peaceful. Unhindered and unbaffled.

"Get on the horse with Jose and follow us. I've never resorted to begging in my entire life, but I am pleading with you to come. You have been wronged. I couldn't reason with Nathan about you, your supposed marriage, bringing you to the Parlor. He dug himself a hole and almost allowed it to bury him," Naomi appealed.

Her head pivoted slowly, sluggishly. Peering at Jose, Amy stressed, "You will stay with me? You can take me there after I pack my things. And, Josie. She must leave too."

Jose nodded. "Whatever you want."

Glen's horse continued stomping and prancing. She would too if she bore the weight of the discord between Glen and Naomi on her back. The angry woman continuously elbowed him in the ribs and slapped his hands if they came anywhere near touching her.

"Go. We will be there," Jose declared. He grabbed her hand and led her inside the Parlor through the kitchen. He took her upstairs and waited outside her door as she tossed the few items she brought with her and a few gifts she had received into her bag. All the gaudy articles provided and purchased for her, she left behind. She had no intention of ever having need of them again.

Handing off the bag to Jose, she hurried to Josie's door and banged on it repeatedly without any response. Jose cleared his throat loudly and she realized someone, or several someones, were climbing the stairs.

Lola and Virgil stepped onto the landing. Lola addressed her, "She too has left. I heard she bailed the Beecher brothers out and is planning to reside at their place."

Whether a good or bad thing, at least she left. Amy would seek her out later and hear from Josie what she hoped and planned for.

"In a few hours I have lost three of my most profitable girls. It is indeed a sad day for me," Lola admitted.

Amy couldn't deny Lola had treated her kindly and fairly. No words came, though. Her emotions were muddled, her thoughts random. They bounced around from Glen, to Naomi, to Lizzie, to the Big G, to Jose.

Unexpectedly, Lola approached and held out her hand. "I hate to lose you. Despite everything, your presence here reminded me of the women and services I initially sought to introduce here. The Parlor is not a saloon. This is an escape for those yearning for satisfying company with discretion. And I thank you."

Accepting Lola's hand, Amy held it. Still, no words came. Lola hugged her detachedly before turning and leaving. Virgil swooped in and embraced her firmly. "It's been a pleasure, Amy. Don't be a stranger. Though I understand if you are."

He departed behind Lola. The tears formed and fell. Should she be happy? Or sad? She experienced both. She couldn't figure it out. She had an eerie sensation of being absent from it all. Hollow.

Lifting her bag in one hand, Jose grasped her hand in the other. "You tell me. I can take you to my aunts' now."

Through everything, Jose remained a constant. He stayed by her side when she sold herself to men for a dinner or conversation. He stayed by her side after learning her role in terminating Lizzie's pregnancy. And he remained. "Let's see this to the end. I can't move forward until I know the truth. The reasoning. And I can't abandon Lizzie or Josie."

A flicker of something she couldn't decipher flashed in his eyes. *Disappointment?* Sure, she should have referenced him in her rationalization, yet she didn't. She married Glen believing he had her best interests at heart. He didn't. Trusting a man again would be difficult. She trusted Jose, but she no longer trusted herself. She no longer knew herself. Trusting again depended on her confidence. Glen shattered it.

"I understand," he responded. He averted her gaze, but he kept his fingers entwined with hers. "Let's go and put this behind us."

Her feet moved along as Jose squeezed her hand in his and led her out and to his horse. Once he secured her bag, he lifted her onto the horse and swung himself up behind her. They rode in silence. She saw nothing. She heard nothing. Her body was obviously present, but nothing else. She and Glen, or Nathan, weren't married. He and Naomi were. For weeks she lived as and among 'fallen women' and gave him most of her earnings. Could she or her reputation ever recover? No one back home need ever know.

Trotting up to the entrance to the Big G where Floyd, Lizzie, Glen aka Nathan, and Naomi waited, she scanned the impressive ranch. It proved to be more than she imagined. Stunning. Beautiful, green land stretched out for as far as the eye could see. A modest, lovely main house rested in the distance with a large barn and a sizable bunkhouse sitting beside it. She recalled seeing the ladies who lived there in town on Saturdays. They always appeared happy and humble. It disheartened her that she gained the opportunity to engage with them, but under the veil of secrecy and shame.

Pinned between Jose's forearms, the tightening of them around her did not go unnoticed. Had he recognized her disquiet? Did he realize she fought the urge to flee?

They rode closer and closer to the home. The tiny orange-haired lady Amy remembered glimpsing in town stepped out on the porch with a miniature version of herself in her arms She thought it might be Laura Garrison. "Clara Mae didn't mention she expected any guests today. I apologize, but she is visiting Mary Catherine and I don't expect her to return until after-noon," she greeted.

Glen tied his horse and helped Naomi down. "We aren't here to see her."

The tiny woman's expression changed from welcoming to concerned. "I am not sure what brings you calling, but I don't suspect it is anything I can offer."

"I've heard Mr. Irving Slater is on the premises. It is him I wish to speak with," Glen declared.

The news apparently rattled the woman. She hugged her child closer to her chest but responded politely, "Please, all of you come in and make yourselves comfortable. I will serve coffee and tea. I also have pie."

It all happened around her. Amy never felt present. Jose basi-cally pulled her off the horse. If he didn't, would she have stayed as she sat? All six of them entered the house. The smells of pies and bread filled the space. The hotel restaurant offered wonderful scents but being in a home with them again made Amy yearn for what she left and what she expected to have. It didn't happen. Now it never would.

An older couple seated at the table stood as they entered. The man addressed Glen, as he walked in first. "I am Irving Slater." He placed his hand on the woman's back. "This is my wife, Marian. I believe I saw you leave the bunkhouse earlier. Is there a problem on the ranch?"

Gesturing to a chair for Naomi, who refused it and stomped away from him, Glen advised, "I would like the rest of you to take a seat. Seems Naomi will not, but I pray the remainder of you do."

Floyd and Lizzie selected two chairs on the opposite side of the table from him. Jose stood behind one also a good distance from Glen and assessed her acceptance of it. Somehow her body conceded, and she sat.

Marian went and attempted to relieve Laura of the baby. "No. If the ranch is affected in any way, I need to know. I choose to stay."

"But the tension. Bea doesn't need it. I will take her to another room," Marian urged.

"I am not tense, Mother. Are you?"

Glen began speaking, "Where to start has abandoned me. I left Kentucky with a brother I never knew I had. A brother I believed to be a good man. I learned later the truth about him. I can't describe the man he revealed to me afterward as good." Glen sank into a chair. Removing his hat and slapping it on the table, he sighed. "Mr. Slater, you knew a woman... Norma Chumley?"

The older man, Irving Slater, still stood. His eyes narrowed and his lips stiffened. "I did. I hired her after my first wife died. She managed the household and looked after my young son... Howard."

"You cared for her?" Glen pressed.

Mr. Slater sat. Sliding his chair up under the table, he peered at Glen in suspicion. "I did. She served as a nurse during the war before accepting a position with me. She had a calling and claimed she would never be satisfied unless she aided those who had been injured or assisted the struggling families."

"I was seven when she died. All my life with her, she promised my father would come for me. You never did. After her death, I lived in the Louisville Baptist Orphan's Home. That's where I met Naomi. We left together when we reached fifteen years of age." Glen wrung his hands in his lap. He kept his head lowered.

"You believe it is I your mother referenced would come for you? Me? Why? I had no knowledge of your existence. If she wished for me to raise her son... I would have," Mr. Slater stated.

Naomi charged the table and slammed her fists on top. "Liar! She promised him she had informed you of his birth. She promised you would come."

Amy started to stand. Lizzie stretched her arm across the table and grasped her wrist. "Stay. As difficult as I know it is, please stay."

Hearing about orphans and about mistreatment to anyone sickened Amy. But Lizzie had lived through it. If she planned to stay, Amy would too.

Shockingly, Marian responded, "I-I was," she stammered, "pregnant and unmarried, without any employment. Irving took pity on me. I acquired a beautiful home. A caring employer. A sad, troubled young boy. Both were missing a woman I condemned for ever leaving them. I hid her letters. I forgot about them. I never read them." She began sobbing. "I never imagined she wrote him about a child. His child. Howard obviously had found them and came here and attacked Laura with his vicious lies and cruel behavior. We told him to be out of the Pennsylvania house when we returned from Laura and Everett's wedding. He must have found the letters."

"You withheld personal letters, Marian," Irving condemned. He dug his elbows into the wood of the table and dropped his forehead into his palms. "I understand. I do. You sought to protect us. But, Marian. This could have all been avoided."

Glen shouted, "My father never came. But my brother did. Naomi and I had someone who loved us. Besides ourselves."

"Until he didn't," interrupted Naomi.

"I swear I had no idea. I never read the letters or knew of their existence. And I apologize that it was Howard and not I who discovered you and located you." Irving rocked his head, scrubbing his face in his hands.

"The first few weeks, he awed us with his educated chatter and his easy wealth. His moods and ideas began to shift. They were erratic. I warned Nathan. I did. But he had a brother. Family. I failed in my attempts to convince him how troubled Howard increasingly became." Naomi stepped behind Nathan and stroked his shoulder. "We both believed his claims that you chose to deny Nathan as your son."

Clasping his hand over Naomi's, Nathan sighed. "After the incident with Glen Jernigan, the doubts started. Once I acquired a job here on the ranch and got to know all of you... I distrusted everything Howard had told me. He assaulted Lizzie. And then he died. I didn't know what to do. I followed him and participated in his absurd schemes. Because he had me hating you, Mr. Irving. And all and anything related to this ranch. He incited in me a desire to retaliate against you all."

"What happened to Glen?" Amy asked.

Chewing on his bottom lip, his eyes went to the floor before settling on her. "Howard told us we were stopping to give the horses a rest and refill our water supply. Glen had your picture on the table. He never stopped talking about you and what he wanted you to have. His excitement and optimism enraged Howard. Stalking up behind the enraptured man as he sat at the table holding your picture, Howard strangled him and snatched the picture on his way out."

Her heart broke. He had shared her enthusiasm of a future together. Tears filled her eyes. "Why pretend to be him? How could you deceive me with a fake wedding?"

Nathan's eyes darted to the floor. "Howard told me to assume his identity. I don't know why. I suspect to conceal the name Chumley until he initiated his revenge plot. He said you would no longer be here when your intended didn't appear and claim you promptly. Once Lizzie saw your photo, we had to adjust to avoid unwanted suspicion. I still can't explain why I kept it."

"Because you have a huge heart. You were led astray by a disturbed brother. He has struggled with the death of Glen. Guilt has plagued him for his treachery to you, Amy." Naomi fixed her eyes on Amy's. Hers too were filled with tears. "We are not bad people. Howard did not spare us any of the grotesque details of the night he took you, Lizzie. Nathan assumed you were with child because I am as well. He noticed comparisons in our appearances and demeanor."

A loud groan captured the attention of them all. Irving closed his eyes and his lips trembled. "Oh, no. Howard. How could you?" he mumbled. Marian went and wrapped her arms around him. "I am horrified." His eyes sprang up. "Lizzie, I-I am devastated. Please, please forgive me."

"You don't require any forgiveness, Mr. Slater. You have not wronged her," Floyd declared.

Nathan cleared his throat forcefully. "Naomi and I will be on our way. Everything is revealed. I regret my actions. I am at peace knowing Howard's child, my future niece or nephew, though conceived in the worst imaginable circumstances, will be born to a loving family and into a supportive community."

"I too am ashamed. This area and the wonderful citizens give me hope that Nathan and I will be lucky enough to live in and raise our baby somewhere as special," Naomi stated.

Laura, rocking the baby in her arms, marched to the center of the table. "This is a lot to comprehend. Almost too much. I suggest no one make any rash decisions. We need to all take some time."

Leaving her chair, Amy's tears came faster. She stopped in front of Jose. "I wish to leave. Please."

Clutching her around the waist, Jose took her out of the house. Away from the culprits who betrayed her. The ones who humiliated and abused her trust. The ones who shredded her heart.

Jose lifted her onto his horse. Once he got in the saddle, he grabbed her and held her against his chest. He whispered in her hair, "It's hard. I understand. You got answers. Your insecurities can be put to rest."

True. But where did she go from there? Did she truly wish to return home? She couldn't. Not until she gained closure. And that started with visiting Glen's home and paying her respects.

Her head and her heart hammered until her entire body ached from the force and exertion it necessitated. Tomorrow. Jose would accompany her. He hadn't disappointed her. Yet. Could she trust he wouldn't?

CHAPTER 13

RACHEL

*T*he plan was in motion. Rachel had only a few misgivings and several mixed emotions. She worried about getting out of town unseen and the worry she would cause her family until she was safely back east and could notify them. She hated to leave the friends she had made and the people at the library. Most of all, she hated to leave Joshua, but it had to be. He was not the right man for her. She was sure of it. Her heart would just have to understand, as would her body. Her mind knew what the right thing to do was and it was telling her to go to Aunt Mary's.

The letter had been posted, she had her bags packed, and now she only had to wait for the perfect time to get away. Her parents had talked of going on a trip to the city to do some shopping for the house, so she hoped that would be soon. That would give her time to get to the train station, purchase a ticket, and be on her way with no one knowing.

As luck would have it, when she returned home from the

library that day, she heard her father telling her mother they would leave the next morning.

At supper that night, her father also told them the Beecher boys had been bailed out of jail by a woman. He looked at Rachel. "Now, dear, while we are gone, I want you to be extremely careful and aware of your surroundings. From what the sheriff told me, he has given the boys a warning to stay away from you. He feels there is no need to be concerned as both boys seemed to be quite close to the woman who came to their aid. She gave her word to the sheriff that she would look out for the Beecher boys and there would be no more issues. Still, do not take any chances with your safety. I trust you now to be able to watch out for yourself. Of course, if you have any problems, you can always call upon Joshua."

At the look she gave him, he added, "Or Conrad and Sarah, of course."

Her mother was more concerned than her father, it seemed. "Should we postpone our trip?" she asked.

"No, Mother, please do not do that on my account. I will be fine. It isn't far to walk to the library, and I am always home before dark. I promise I will be alert and careful when I am out."

"You heard the girl, dear. I believe she has learned her lesson," her father added.

After she had helped with the supper dishes, she excused herself and went up to her room to pack a few last-minute items. Carefully stowing her bags under the bed, she sat down on the edge and thought about what her father had told her. *It really is good for me to leave, now that those awful boys are out of jail. That will be the reason I give everyone once they realize I am gone.*

It really couldn't have happened at a better time. Tomorrow, she would make her excuses at work, then head to the train station. It couldn't be simpler.

The next morning, she said goodbye to her parents, giving both of them an extra-long hug. "Have a wonderful time and don't worry about me. I'll be fine," she said as she walked to the door with them.

She hurriedly got ready for work. Once at the library, she asked to speak to Mrs. Richards in private. The woman ushered her into her office.

"Is everything all right, dear?" the kindly woman asked.

Rachel hesitated. She really hated to leave this wonderful woman. She had grown to love her and her work. But she forced herself to say, "I'm afraid something has come up, and I must go away for a while. I am so sorry to leave you short-handed, but it is something I really must do."

"I understand. Things sometimes come up. This wouldn't have anything to do with the release of the Beecher boys, now would it?"

Rachel knew she was blushing when she replied, "As a matter of fact, it does. I just feel it would be better if I left town for a bit. My parents have gone to the city for a few days, and I will be visiting my au… er, a friend."

"Of course, dear. Don't you worry a bit. Your job will be here for you when you return. I have a few volunteers who can fill your shifts until then."

Guilt nudged at her as she said, "Thank you, ma'am. I do appreciate your concern and understanding."

"Now, why don't you run along and get started on your trip? I can manage today."

"Are you sure you don't wish for me to work my shift today?"

"I think it best if you get on your way. Things will die down here, and you can return soon."

"Yes, ma'am," Rachel said as she hugged Mrs. Richards.

She hurried home then and grabbed her bags, making sure she had enough money for the trip in her reticule. She really should stop by and see Sarah, but it was too risky. She walked the short distance to the livery, taking the back streets, her senses on alert. Once she had secured a ride to the station, she breathed a sigh of relief.

At the station, she was able to purchase a ticket for the train that was scheduled to leave in one hour. She sat on a bench away from the other passengers, her head down so as not to draw attention to herself. When she was finally seated on the train, she was able to relax a bit. A sudden wave of sadness overwhelmed her and she very nearly got off the train, but that little voice in the back of her mind told her to stay, that she was doing the right thing, the only thing she could. She needed to put distance between herself and Mr. Joshua Thomas. It was the only way she would ever have any peace of mind. Her parents would be shocked, worried, and then angry, she was sure. But they would eventually understand. She hoped so, anyway. And Sarah, well, she might never understand, but she and her sister were not alike in many respects. Sarah belonged here. She did not. It was as simple as that. She hoped her aunt had received her letter and was expecting her. They had a lot to catch up on.

The train finally departed the station and as she looked out the window, a tear fell down her cheek. This was what she wanted. It was what she had planned since the day she had arrived in Oklahoma, the day she left Philadelphia, actually. So why was she sad? She knew the answer to that question, but she refused to acknowledge it.

"Goodbye, Joshua," she said as the train left town.

It would take several days to get back east. Her parents would be home before she arrived in Philadelphia, but there would be enough miles between them by that time that they wouldn't be able to catch up with her soon. Would they come after her? If so, could she convince them to allow her to stay back east? Well, she would worry about that if the time came. For now, she planned to relax. She pulled out a book she had brought with her and began to read.

"Good morning," a deep voice said.

Rachel looked up. "Hello." The man seated across from her wasn't bad looking, but he was no match for Joshua. She had to stop doing that! She could not go through the rest of her life comparing every man she met to him.

"Are you going east?" the man asked.

"Visiting family," she replied noncommittally.

"Ah, I see. I am heading to New York myself. I have a job opportunity there."

"Good luck to you," she said and returned to her reading, hoping he would realize she wasn't in the mood for chatting.

"Thank you. I will leave you to your book. If you need any assistance during the trip, please call upon me. I would be happy to be of service. I know it can be hard for a woman to travel alone."

"Thank you," she said with a smile.

She read for several hours and then it was time for a break. She got off the train with the other passengers and went inside the station where there was a small café. After ordering food, she sat alone and started to eat her meal.

"May I join you?" It was the man from the train again.

"Of course," she said. He really was a nice sort, or he seemed to be. Perhaps a bit of flirting would be fun. *No, Rachel, absolutely not. Your plan is working so far. Stick to it.*

He made casual conversation, never saying anything to indicate that he was interested in anything other than a companion on the trip. It was just as well. She did learn that his name was Curtis Morrow and he was to take a job in New York with a law firm. He had been practicing law for a while in Oklahoma but relatives in the east had told him of the opportunity and he had jumped on it. He had been a judge for the last year in Oklahoma but would be an attorney in his new position. He told her he had always dreamed of going to New York City.

"I hope it is all you wish it to be," Rachel said. "I have only been in Oklahoma a short time. My family moved out west to be near my sister and her husband."

"I see. Well, it is time to reboard the train. Shall I escort you?"

"That would be nice. Thank you," she said politely.

As the train moved along the tracks, she thought about Curtis Morrow. He was an attorney. He would be living in New York City. Maybe she should consider him more seriously. He was, after all, much more suited for her than Joshua.

But when she felt a pang in her heart at the thought, she quickly dismissed it.

When nightfall came, she made her way to the ladies' water closet to get ready for the night. She returned to her seat and got comfortable with the pillow and blanket provided and attempted to sleep. It wasn't as comfortable as having a car to herself with a bunk, but she had tried to economize. She was finally able to get comfortable and closed her eyes.

WHEN RACHEL'S parents had returned home to find her gone, her mother panicked. George tried to put her mind at ease by alerting Sarah, Conrad and Joshua and asking them all to meet to discuss her disappearance before making any rash decisions. As he left Conrad's office, he swung by the library to ask Mrs. Richards if she knew where his daughter had gone.

"Mr. Linton, how lovely to see you. How was your trip to the city?" the woman greeted him.

"Ah, my daughter must have told you we were away for a few days," he answered, hoping to steer the conversation to Rachel quickly.

"Yes, she did. Did she arrive at her friend's safely? I must say I believe she made a wise decision."

"Mrs. Richards, would you please elaborate? I am afraid Rachel did not tell us she was leaving or where she was headed."

"Oh my, I am surprised. Rachel is such a responsible young woman. Well, let me see. She left three days ago, I believe. Said she was going to visit a friend because of the Beecher boys being let out of jail. She told me you and your wife had gone to the city for a few days."

"I see. Well, I guess she was more upset by that news than she let on to us. Do you happen to know the name of the friend she went to visit?"

"I am sorry, she didn't say. Is there anything I can do to help? I assured her that she would still have her job on her return. She did not give me a timeframe, I'm afraid."

"Thank you, Mrs. Richards, you have been very helpful. If you remember anything else, please let me know."

"Of course, yes."

By the time he arrived home, his wife, Sarah, Conrad, and Joshua were seated at the kitchen table drinking coffee and talking.

"I have some news," George said as he joined them. He relayed to them what the librarian had told him.

"Hmm, do you really think that is why she left?" Joshua asked. "It may have been a factor in the timing, but she did tell me she intended to go back east. She was not happy here."

Everyone looked at him in surprise. "She wasn't happy?" Sarah asked. "I thought she was finally adjusting. She seemed to like her work and had made some friends. She was even learning to bake."

Conrad said, "I think she has had her mind set on going back east all along, like Joshua said. Do any of you have any idea who this friend is she has gone to?"

"I don't know. It could be anyone. Maybe we should get in touch with Mary." Mrs. Linton looked at her husband. "Send her a wire? Maybe she has heard from Rachel."

"My guess is that is exactly where she has gone, to Mary's,"

George said glumly. "The exact person we were trying to steer her away from."

"Mary is my father's sister," Sarah explained to Conrad and Joshua.

"Yes, George has mentioned that he thought she was a bad influence on Rachel," Conrad said.

Joshua had been quiet, listening. Finally, he spoke up. "Sir, I would like your permission to go after her." He looked at George.

"You have it."

"Yes, please do that," Sarah and her mother said in unison.

"Shall I go with you?" Conrad asked.

"No. Thank you for offering, but I think this is something I need to handle on my own. I would also like permission to make her my wife before I bring her back." Again, he looked to George for his approval.

Mr. Linton looked at his wife and she nodded. "All right, son. If you think you can convince her to marry you and come back here, you have both of our blessings."

"Thank you. Also, the time has come for you to know the truth. I have been keeping it under wraps until the time is right, and I think that time is now." He looked over at Conrad before going on. "When my grandfather passed, I received a substantial inheritance. I chose to come back here, rather than stay on at my family's firm. I used part of that money to buy into Conrad's company. I have been a silent partner in Appleby Oil all this time. I was working as a roughneck in order to learn the business from the ground up. The only people who were aware of this were Conrad and Sarah, of course, and Clyde, our driller. Another reason was that I am in love with your daughter. I wanted Rachel to love me for myself and not because I was a business owner. Maybe I was wrong not to tell her the truth."

"Um, this is news," George said. "I can understand your

reasons, but it is good that it is out in the open now. Congratulations."

"Yes, congratulations," Rosella added.

"There is more," Joshua said. "I am the new owner of Mr. Ryan's house. A room has opened up at the boarding house and he is moving this week. I wonder if I might impose upon the two of you," he looked at Sarah and Rosella, "to make it ready for Rachel and me while I am gone to fetch her."

"Goodness, now that is a surprise," Sarah said. "Even I didn't know that. Of course, I will help."

"How lovely it will be to have you next door. Mr. Ryan is a dear and it was very good of you to let him stay on until he was able to get a room," Rosella said.

"I should get to the bunkhouse and pack my things. I'll try to leave on today's train." Joshua stood and shook Mr. Linton's hand, then he said to Conrad, "You okay while I am gone? Anything I need to take care of at the office before I go?"

"We're good. You just bring that wayward sister-in-law of mine home." Conrad slapped Joshua on the back. "Good luck."

After he left to pack, George sent a wire to his sister in Philadelphia, informing her that they believed Rachel was headed her way. He also told her that Joshua was following and not to tell Rachel he was coming. He grinned as he walked home from the telegraph office. Oh, how he wished he could be a fly on the wall when the young man arrived.

RACHEL ARRIVED on her aunt's doorstep, tired and ready for a bath and a bed. She rang the bell, hoping Aunt Mary was home and that she had received her letter.

The door opened and her aunt pulled her inside and into a hug. "Oh, my dear girl. You should have wired to let me know when your train got in. I would have picked you up, but your letter was so vague. Let me get a good look at you."

"Well, I am here now, Auntie. I was so worried I would arrive before my letter did."

"I think my girl would like a nice hot bath. Am I right? I'll fix us a meal and we can talk after you've had a chance to relax in that big tub of mine."

"That sounds heavenly," Rachel hastily agreed.

"Take your things to your regular room and help yourself to anything."

Rachel went up the stairs and put her things in the first bedroom on the right. It was the room she always stayed in when at her aunt's house. Then she grabbed a fresh dress and headed to the elaborate water closet to soak in the huge clawfoot tub. She added scented bath salts to the warm water and swished them around with her hand before stripping out of her dusty clothes and sinking into the wonderfully warm water.

She soaked for a while before scrubbing the dirt and grime off her body and hair. Then she got dressed and went downstairs to join her aunt.

"Just in time. Sit and have a cup of tea. The pot is on the table. I'll bring the soup and bread over and we can catch up while we have a bite."

Rachel helped herself to tea, added sugar and cream and took a sip. Her aunt brought chicken soup to the table and once they had filled their bowls and buttered thick slices of bread, they began to talk.

"Tell me, what brings you back? Is this a visit or do you intend to stay?" her aunt asked cautiously, not giving anything away that she already knew from her brother.

"I am hoping to stay. I, well, the west just wasn't right for me. My folks are doing well there, and Sarah loves it, but I miss the social life here."

"I was so hoping you would meet a nice young man out there," Mary said.

"I am surprised to hear you say that, Aunt Mary. I mean, you enjoy the social scene yourself. You haven't remarried in all these years."

"Oh, my dear, it isn't for lack of wanting to find a good man. There are just none around here who have caught my fancy."

Rachel was again surprised. "I-I had no idea. I am so sorry you have found no one if that is the case."

"Now, tell me about your new home. Enough about me."

"Well, the house is very nice. My bedroom has a window seat just like the one I had in my bedroom in our house here. I met some nice folks, and I was working a few days a week at the local library."

"I haven't heard anything so far that explains why you feel it isn't the place for you, my dear," her aunt said kindly before she took a spoonful of soup to her lips.

"Well, um, there was a young man, but it just could never be. H-he wasn't the right man for me."

"And why is that, dear?"

"Well, his name is Joshua. He is from here, actually. He comes from a wonderful family, a business family. But instead of joining the family firm, he chose to go out west and work as a... a laborer. First, as a ranch hand and more recently as a roughneck on one of Sarah's husband's oil rigs." She shuddered.

"What is wrong with that? He sounds like a very industrious young man. He could have had his life planned out for him, but he chose to make it on his own. There is nothing wrong with manual labor and hard work, Rachel. I am surprised at you."

"Aunt Mary, I thought you, of all people, would understand my concerns. I should be with a man who... who is into the social set, one who works at a reputable job in a business environment."

Aunt Mary laughed. "Oh, sweet Rachel, you have a lot to

learn. Don't you know that most of the men like you are describing are full of themselves, they think they can do no wrong, they take mistresses after they are married, and they think their money can buy them anything they want? I would much prefer a man such as the one you described. I am so sorry if I did you the injustice of leading you to believe otherwise. I do enjoy social gatherings, but if I had my druthers, I would be married and living a quiet life. It just hasn't happened for me."

Rachel was stunned. "I-I had no idea. May I stay, though? I-I do not know what to do."

"Tell me more about Joshua. Are you in love with him?"

Rachel hesitated and took a bite of bread before answering. Chewing slowly, she finally swallowed and said, "I-I do not know. My heart says yes, but my mind says he is not right for me."

"Follow your heart, dear girl. Your mind is set on a certain lifestyle, but you will never be happy settling for a man you do not love. Was it really so bidding in Oklahoma? It sounded to me as if you were starting to settle in when you left."

"I have known since the day I left here that I wanted to come back. My mind was made up. And then, there was the attack. At a church social, two young men accosted me. Luckily, Joshua and some other men rescued me before any damage could be done. The men were put in jail but were released the day before I got on the train to come back here."

"Oh, dear, how frightening. But if Joshua came to your rescue, he must have feelings for you as well. I feel he would protect you."

"H-he does have feelings for me, or at least he did. But I told him it could never work. It is too late."

"Sweetheart, it is never too late. Now, why don't you run on upstairs and unpack and get some rest? You are welcome to stay with me as long as you wish, but please give some serious thought to the things we have talked about. We will talk more tomorrow."

"Yes, ma'am. Are you sure I can't help you clear up first?"

"I've got it. You get some rest."

So, Rachel went up to her room and put her things away before getting ready for bed. Once settled in the comfortable bed under the covers, she thought about all the things her aunt had said. To think all this time, she was under the impression her aunt was happy with her life. How wrong she had been. Perhaps she should just pack up Aunt Mary and take her back to Oklahoma with her.

What a crazy thought. I must be really tired.

 *my*

DISGUSTING AND DISAPPOINTING. Her. Her life. What the heck happened? And she permitted it. All of it. It appalled her. No excuses she fathomed could alleviate her acceptance and partici-pation. She suspected. She recognized the avoidance Glen/Nathan, issued. She realized the compromising situation he placed her in at the Parlor. Yet, she concurred. Did it say more about him? Or her?

Declining Jose's persistent invitation to stay with his aunts, she intended to go to the hotel and impose on Ruth's hospitality again. But as she entered the lobby, while Jose carried her bag behind her, Iva, the hotel owner's wife, greeted her from behind the registration desk.

"Amy, everyone has missed you more than you know. I can't help but notice your bag. I hope this means you are coming back to us. Mrs. Wilson especially missed you. The restaurant and the hotel are overflowing with guests." She leaned into and over the desk and divulged, "Pearl, the timid thing she hired after you, just up and left the other day in a tizzy of tears and blubbering."

"I hate to hear that," Amy remarked. And she did. She adored Mrs. Wilson and disliked knowing the poor lady had even less help after asking her to take some shifts and Amy stalled in committing herself. The opportunity passed. One she enjoyed. It gave her satisfaction performing basic skills amongst wonderful people while engaging with others. Accepting it now would bring shame and gossip to the wholesome and communal establishment. She allowed Nathan to place her in objectionable and ostracized situations.

Stupid of her to imagine she could take employment someplace other than the factory once she returned home. Living under her father's roof, admitting her failure in her naïve dreams of marrying and living happily with a man she never met in a place she had never been, followed by the shame of a sham of a marriage—devastated and damaged her. Pa would insist she abandon her immature fancies and acknowledge the good life they had and cease her derision of it. More regrets for her to bear. She disrespected her parents. Her chest tightened recalling their arguments and how she boasted about leaving there and the fabulous life she would have in Oklahoma.

Deciding to treat herself and not take advantage of Ruth, she told Iva she desired a room for the night. And a hot bath. She no longer needed the money she saved. Soon enough, she would be home and working alongside her parents. They weren't wealthy. But they had enough to live comfortably and never wanted for anything. She would adopt their perspectives. Whatever earnings remained after she left, she would happily give to them. The time had come for her to resign herself to reality. Besides her parents' expectation of her conceding to take a position at the factory and offering her pay to assist in funding the household, things could be worse. A lot worse.

In a few hours out of one day, she heard unimaginable stories. Even before then, Lizzie had cried to her and begged for help because she carried the child of her attacker. Nathan and Naomi grew up in an orphanage. Howard Slater affected a lot of lives negatively. So, Amy couldn't complain.

The pain she witnessed in Jose's beautiful face imprinted on her. Forever. No doubt. His kind, brown eyes peered into hers. They questioned. They pleaded. Whether or not the fault started with Nathan, she couldn't claim innocence. She tempted men and accepted payment for her company. It sickened her. Jose deserved better. She could never justify abusing his unconditional affection. If she continued with him, it would be abuse.

No, she couldn't feign ignorance any longer. Nathan confessed everything. She must take responsibility for herself. She behaved as a coward. A follower. Ignoring her intuition. It shamed her beyond comprehension.

"I am not comfortable leaving you," Jose stated.

"I know." Creases of tension in his forehead and the reluctance in his gaze supported his admission, but she would do right by him. Even if it broke her heart and she would never recover, she must leave him. "I appreciate your concern, but I need to be alone."

He nodded and sighed. "I am sure Clyde and Joshua will be livid when I return to the site in the morning. Floyd, Nathan, nor I reported in at the drill site today. As soon as I am released tomorrow, I will come straight here."

She should advise him not to. Circling her eyes from the ceiling to the floor, she stammered, "Can... can I ask one more thing of you? I know I shouldn't."

"Anything. Anytime." He reached out and cupped her cheek, tilting her face and encouraging her to look at him. He grinned. It appeared forced, but his eyes reassured her.

"If you see Nathan, ask for directions to Glen's. I wish to pay my respects." Her chin quivered and his fingers slid down her face and he rubbed his thumb across it.

"Of course."

He turned and left her standing in the lobby. She fought the urge to call him back. But she couldn't be selfish. She planned to go and never see him again. It made no difference if she shared his affection and attraction. And she did. His touch created a surge of emotion and desire in her. His animated stories amused and captivated her. But it couldn't be.

"If I didn't know better, I think that Mexican harbors intense feelings for you. Best you distance yourself from him and his kind," Iva remarked.

Never would Amy refuse him because of his heritage. She was the one he should refuse. "I am going to forget you said that. He is Lizzie's relative. And unless you are a liar, she is a close friend of yours," Amy snapped.

Iva jolted as if she'd been struck with a large rock. Her eyes went wide, and her mouth fell. "She is. I regret my comment."

"I certainly hope so." Lifting her bag, Amy snatched the room key from Iva's hand and went to the staircase.

After a hot bath, Amy stretched out on the bed. It engulfed her. Or everything did. She curled up on one side and buried her head into the pillow and under the bedcovers. Sleep seized her. She awoke to blaring sunshine spilling inside the window and across the floor. She heard nothing except the usual chatter between hotel guests and personnel as they strolled the hallway. She certainly didn't feel capable of being seen or interacting with anyone.

It's not as if she could remain in there forever. But the prospect sure appealed to her. What harm could it do for one day? She had nowhere to be. At least not until she learned where Glen resided during his life and now in death. She stayed in bed. She slept. She sobbed. She sobbed more. She slept more.

It shocked her when knocking at the door had her throwing

the pillow and covers from her head and she noticed the room had grown darker. Rays of sunlight no longer entered through the window. Shuffling from the bed, she shoved her arms in her night coat and lit a lamp.

Opening the door enough to view the individual on the other side, she saw Jose. He had a swollen, split lip, multiple scratches and cuts on his face, and one bruised eye. Flinging the door wider, she gripped his wrist, attempting to pull him inside her room.

He shook free. "I can't come inside, Amy. I am fine." Shoving his hand in his pocket, he pulled out a piece of paper. "Nathan drew a map of Glen's location... his residence and where he and Naomi buried him. Before I jumped the deceitful bastard. He got in a few good licks, but he's in a lot worse condition."

"You were fighting? Jose... you shouldn't have."

"Like hell I shouldn't have. He's lucky he still breathes." A couple exited the room across the hall and watched him and her in curious fascination as they slowly sauntered away. "Have you stayed in here all day? In bed?" he quizzed. The sternness in his tone and the menacing disapproval in his glare advised her that the thought of such displeased him.

"I had nowhere to be. No one to see," she countered.

There was a tic in his jaw and he grumbled, "I see. So, I am no one to you now."

"You know that's not what I meant. I didn't realize the late hour."

"Of course, you didn't. Because you never left the bed. I rushed directly here after my shift. I had to see you and know you were all right. I am filthy from working and bloody from brawling with Nathan." He stood awaiting a response. She had none. "Several of the roughnecks got displaced to other ranches today. And they assigned me the night shift. After I clean up and do some chores on the farm, I will be back here at seven in the morning for breakfast. Please meet me downstairs at the restaurant."

He continued to stare at her. She stared back at him. If he required an affirmation to his request, they might possibly be there a while. Being an obedient woman had not served her well.

"Okay then, Amy. I hope you join me. Especially since I have an additional shift with a crew and at a rig unfamiliar to me in a few hours."

She sighed and rolled her eyes. He turned and marched away.

Good. They shouldn't spend any time together.

Shutting the door, her knees buckled, and she wailed. Never being around him again, never hearing his laugh, never experiencing his touch, shattered her. She crawled to the bed and climbed onto it. The tears came in torrents. Her body tremored. One would expect that reaction after the duplicity Glen executed. But it came from her passionate feelings and heartbreak over losing Jose.

Sometime after she cried until her eyes went dry and her throat ached, she drifted into a troubled slumber. The incessant thumping of her aching heart pounded in her ears refusing her the peace she longed for. To let her be. She understood she continued to live. It astounded her how. Her exterior form lingered. Her interior decomposed. All except her mangled heart. It hammered until she burst into a seated position with her hands over her ears.

"Amy, open the door," Jose demanded. She sensed he was frantic. Springing out of the bed, she opened the door and he darted inside and slammed it behind him. "I waited almost an hour. I am exhausted. I can't see straight. I can't think clearly." He hurled his hat onto the floor and stomped around it. Pausing, he brought a hand to his brow and swiped it in obvious disgust before resuming his tramping.

"Why can't you leave me be? There is a woman worthy of you." The statement brought tears she believed she'd expended to her eyes. She cocked her head and jerked it upright in a flash. The odd movement and urge to repeat it possessed her. As did the absurdity and madness of it. Thinking of another woman tending to him and he to another woman, incapacitated her.

"Do you believe I need to be punished?" he asked.

"No. Never. Me. I need to be punished," she replied.

"For what, I can't comprehend. You don't believe I need to be punished and yet you keep punishing me. Why? Because you convicted yourself for some crime you didn't commit and won't move beyond it. I'll intervene. Nathan is guilty. I will never pardon Nathan. The facts are the facts, Amy. It could've been worse. He denied you consummation. He minimized your involvement in any public capacity to reduce any scrutiny. And no," he thundered as he clutched her hip, plopped into the chair, and yanked her over his knees, "I will never forgive him for not adoring you, and flaunting you, and indulging you as any man who ever had the extraordinary opportunity to do so should. And I, by the Lord's grace, received one. So, if you wish to be punished, I will deliver it."

Only the truly demented wished for a punishment, so she concluded she truly was demented. Being over his lap and willingly vulnerable to him under no duress except self-inflicted, mended cracks within her. There were obvious sections not fully broken. They were the portions Jose owned. Only him. "I am a travesty. I should be punished."

"If you say so," he retorted. His palm slammed onto her backside. Over and over. He spanked her. Unforgivingly. The stings invaded her without mercy. The smacks seared her from outside inwardly. And she cried in unison with her pleas for more.

With each strike, she embraced the agony. She absorbed it and luxuriated in it. It displaced the mental anguish consuming her and she ejected it with each smack.

He delivered a dozen or more strikes to one cheek before switching to the other and repeating the action. He reduced the number and began alternating single or double slaps between both.

The burning and stinging subsided. She welcomed it and immersed herself in it—wholly. She prayed it would incinerate the weakened and corrupted facets of her being.

Beyond her awareness, the punishment ceased. Enveloped in peace, engulfed in silence, she inhaled a weightless breath. She swallowed easily.

All because of Jose. He gave her what she needed. Again.

Twisting over his knees, she grasped his shoulders, jerked her night garments up to her knees, and straddled him. Caressing his face, she threaded her fingers in his dark hair and tugged him forward until his lips met hers.

She knew after the blissfulness diminished, she would once again have no more to lose and no more to give. In those moments, she received a reprieve. She could give and take and suspend her suffering. Because she was empty.

She kissed him as if her life depended on it. She kissed him as if she would never taste him again. Trailing his hand from her side to her neck, he guided her head back, exposing her throat to him. He licked and sucked and kissed it. It aroused her beyond her wildest imaginations. Her breasts became heavy. She snatched at his shirt until she freed his hard torso. He tore open her thin night garments and pressed his bare chest into hers. She gasped. Splaying his fingers, he clutched her naked back and held her tightly. She swore her body melted into his.

"We can't do this. We must stop," he declared. His voice sounded hoarse and pained.

Instinctively, her hips rocked against his. She didn't want to stop. He could soothe her discomfort.

"Don't say that," she muttered into his jaw before claiming his mouth again.

His hands caressed her back. His tongue danced with hers.

Her hips rocked again, and he groaned, "We can wait until we marry."

Marry. That would never happen. But damn if she would say or do anything to break the spell that they were under. One of his hands slid from her back and massaged one of her breasts. Her center throbbed, and she ground into him and clawed at his back.

"Please, Jose. Take me and satisfy this yearning you have produced," she urged.

Startlingly, and in a swift and uncoordinated motion, he stood and deposited her on the bed. She first thought he intended to give her what she asked. He did not.

Gripping the hem of her shift, he wrenched it down her legs, concealing them. "I mention us marrying and you say nothing," he barked. "You lay up in this bed and disregard my invitation for breakfast. You wallow in your misery and confess your need to be punished—" He fisted his hands and shook them in the air. "I cannot contribute to any act you will undoubtedly decide is sinful and necessitate additional redemption."

She didn't understand what had him so angry. But his reaction sure made her angry. "If that's how you feel... I apologize for assuming you would have sex with me. And I won't impose on you ever again with my desire to receive a spanking." It's not as if she planned it. It's not as if she ever considered it.

"Amy, I love you and want you to be my wife," he professed.

"You are being silly. Everyone believes I am married. And I am leaving for Virginia once I handle a few matters."

He muttered a bunch of words in what must have been Spanish. It didn't require a translator to know they weren't pleasant. Taking his shirt from the floor, he rammed his head and arms into it. "You are fooling yourself. News travels fast in this area. Nathan and Naomi are living together as the husband and wife they are at the Pendergrass farm. He is working the rig there, and lucky for them, the Pendergrasses took pity on them. After a few weeks, no one will remember this scandal and will have moved on to another one."

Maybe so. But she would always remember it. It would force her to live wondering if others were judging her and speaking about her behind her back. They would refer to her as the dumb mail-order bride so gullible and desperate for a husband she participated in a fake marriage and reduced herself to working at the Parlor per his wishes. The few friends she had would desert her. She would have Jose, or so he claimed. But he would tire of it too. His family and friends would abandon him. He would resent her in the end. He lived under prejudice and as an outsider already. Damn if she would augment it.

Because she loved him. Because she loved him, she would spare him added chagrin.

"I've been selfish and impatient. I want you as my wife, but I sure didn't envision proposing to you today or under these circumstances. But damn, you got me all crazed with desire. And unless I know you will be my wife, I can't claim what isn't mine to take," he emphasized. The tension in his body, face, and tone departed. The man who delighted her with his handsome features and fun stories and never discontinued his friendship or caring attentiveness because of her marital status or her profession stood before her.

If she believed her heart broke before—she again had been naïve. He had appointed himself her protector. She must protect him. Marrying any man seemed improbable and preposterous. She came to marry Glen. A man she would never meet. A man who spoke about her and their future while holding her photograph as an evil man strangled him.

She couldn't conceive a future of love and happiness. Not yet. Probably never.

"I am tired. I wish to sleep," she stated.

"Look out the door and confirm I can leave without notice. I'm tired too. On Saturday I can take you to Glen's. It's a half a day's ride. So, take an entire day there and back. You can leave word at the desk if you choose to go Saturday and have me escort you. I can come by in the morning and check for your message." His dark eyes were laden in sadness.

Hurtling out of the bed, she couldn't bear to observe the turmoil reflected in his eyes, she clutched his hat from the floor and went for the door. Cracking it and peeking out, she saw an empty hallway. "It is clear. Thank you. The concern you have demonstrated to me and for me over and over is extraordinary and I am forever thankful."

He approached slowly and took his hat. "I don't suspect I will have any note from you. If you share any of my affection, do not go alone, Amy." He placed his hand on her head. She turned away from him.

HOW MANY TEARS can one person cry? How long can one wail until sleep seizes them, weakened by fatigue? In and out of those episodes through the day, she momentarily located 'hope'. A hesitant knock came at the door. She sprang from the bed and attempted to straighten her knotted hair with her fingers. Jose came back. He didn't lose faith in her. She had lost all faith, until those seconds believing he returned.

Opening the door, she encountered Iva's round face. "Sorry to disturb you. I have not seen you since you checked in. You reserved and paid one night for your room. This is the third," she notified her.

The sorrow over discovering Jose hadn't returned rendered her speechless and dazed. She had spent two nights and two days in her room. In bed. Howard Slater and Nathan Chumley stole her fiancé, months from her life, and her dignity. Damn if she'd surrender anything else.

Her stomach growled, prompting her to respond. "I apologize. I am going to dress and come down to handle my bill and eat."

"Thank you. I'll see you shortly," Iva replied.

Quickly washing, Amy glanced at herself in the mirror. An Amy she didn't recognize peered back at her. Her blonde hair appeared dull and ratty. The sunken, red eyes and irritated nose also substantiated the despairing state she had sunk into. As did the aches and noises her stomach produced as a reminder that she hadn't eaten anything since Monday. Since the evening meal she shared with Jose.

Managing the best that she could considering the marginal motivation she possessed, she settled her bill, advising Iva she intended to leave in the morning. Wandering into the restaurant oblivious to everything around her, she heard someone call her name.

Mr. Ramsey stood at a table ahead of her. He smiled and waved. "Amy, join me. I insist."

Oddly, seeing him out in public awed her. He confided to her that he hadn't been away from his house except for his Thursdays at the Parlor since his wife left him after the accident. His smile brought one to her face.

They had a wonderful meal and engaging conversation. He confessed that she provided his incentive for venturing into the public establishment. Learning that she would no longer visit with him on Thursday night at the Parlor inspired him to dare beyond it and hopefully maintain a friendship with her. He congratulated her for leaving it and swore he would never mention it to anyone and never again to her.

She had a true friend in him. It impacted her. She had a good Thursday evening after the traumatic Tuesday which altered her forever. A Tuesday that tested her personal ethics. It demolished her confidence. It desecrated her expectations in herself and in others. It modified her ambition and her optimism.

"I pray you will accept my invitation to dinner next Thursday," said Mr. Ramsey as he pushed away from and rounded the table before pulling her chair out.

"I would be delighted," Amy accepted.

She allowed him to escort her out before she searched out Mrs. Wilson. Mrs. Wilson served them, but she had handled all the tables and uncharacteristically conversed minimally with the patrons, and Amy wished to speak to her privately. Entering the kitchen, she saw her frantically dishing plates and scurrying from one side of the space to the other.

"Let me get a few of these for you," offered Amy. "If you are still interested in my help, I'm anxious to return Saturday."

Mrs. Wilson dropped her arms, the plates clattering on the counter, and hugged her. "Thank the Lord. Yes. Yes," she squealed.

"No, thank you," Amy stressed. She delivered meals to several tables and observing the return of Mrs. Wilson's usual smile and congenial conversations with the customers, she left and went to Ruth's room. It took four sets of rapping on the door until it opened. Ruth's hair hung loose, and her cheeks were flushed. Had she been asleep? Not that she didn't deserve rest. She put in long hours working as the hotel's launderess.

"Oh no, I've disturbed you. I hope it's not presumptuous of me, but I have a huge favor to ask," Amy blurted.

"Honey, you can ask anything of me." The sounds of movement inside the room had Ruth squeezing the door closed, leaving only her face squished in the narrow opening. "Now is not a good time. Can we speak in the morning?"

Did Ruth have a guest? It never crossed Amy's mind that Ruth entertained a man. Not because she wasn't attractive. And everyone loved her.

It embarrassed Amy how insensitively she behaved, but her request couldn't wait. "Is there any way possible you can accompany me for a day trip tomorrow? I must make a visit a half day's ride from here. I hate to do it alone."

"I will. What time should I meet you in the lobby?" Ruth answered abruptly.

"Seven. We shouldn't travel at night and that will have us back before sundown. I will have Mrs. Wilson prepare us something to eat." It relieved her beyond words that Ruth agreed.

"I'll be there," Ruth assured, snapping the door shut.

CHAPTER 15

RACHEL

*R*achel and her aunt were in the parlor sipping tea when the doorbell rang five days later.

"Stay there, I'll get it, dear," Aunt Mary said as she stood and left the room. When she returned, she was accompanied by a young man. "Rachel, you have a visitor."

"I do?" Rachel asked, surprised. She looked up and into the eyes of the man she loved. "Joshua!" She couldn't tell if he was angry or relieved.

"Good afternoon, Rachel," he said. "I hope I am not intruding. I've come to take you home."

"I-I am home," she said quietly.

"I have some things to do in the kitchen. You will stay for supper, won't you, Joshua?"

"I would like that, ma'am. I do need to go to my hotel to clean up first. But I would like to speak with your niece alone first if I may?"

"Of course. I'll just be in the kitchen." Mary left the room with a grin on her face.

When she was gone, Joshua looked at Rachel. "May I sit?"

"Suit yourself. Just don't get the furniture dirty."

He ignored her remark and sat down across from her. "What on earth were you thinking, leaving like that without a note for your parents? You could have at least told Sarah where you were going."

"Why? So she could try to stop me?"

He helped himself to a cup of tea before replying. After taking a sip, Joshua said, "I am trying very hard not to be angry with you, young lady. I understand you being upset about the Beecher boys. But my gut tells me you were planning this trip regardless. But to go off without a word to anyone is very irresponsible."

"Mrs. Richards knew I was leaving."

"Thank God for that."

"Do my parents know you are here?"

"Yes, and I am here with their blessing," he said.

"If you think I am going back there, you are—"

Her words were cut off as Joshua stood, came over to her and jerked her up. His lips descended on hers in a kiss that spoke of passion, dominance, anger, and desire.

"Now, you were saying?" he asked when he let her go.

"I said if you think—"

Again, he cut her off but this time with words. "You will come back with me. And furthermore, you will come back as my wife. This nonsense has gone on long enough, Rachel. I love you, and you love me. There is no reason under the sun we shouldn't be together. Your mixed-up notions of the man you should marry are just that. Mixed-up notions."

"Who do you think you are, coming into my aunt's home and ordering me around like this? I've already told you I can't marry you."

"But you didn't really mean it. Now, this is what is going to happen. I am going to go back to my hotel and get cleaned up after the long train ride. Then I will come back for supper with you and your aunt. Tomorrow, we will go see my family. In the next few days, we will get married, spend a few days here, and then catch the train back home. Am I making myself clear?"

Rachel just stared at him, wide-eyed and open-mouthed. Her mind was in a turmoil. Her heart and her body were screaming, "Yes," but her mind wasn't sure. Could she go back to Oklahoma with him, as his wife? Did she want that?

"I will return. In the meantime, think about what I said." He kissed her again and left her standing in the middle of the room, speechless.

A few minutes later, her aunt walked in. "Has Joshua gone? What did he say, dear?"

"Um, uh, well, he said we are getting married and going back to Oklahoma."

"I see," Mary said with a grin. "And what do you think about that?"

"He has a lot of nerve, coming in here and ordering me around like that," Rachel sputtered.

"Now, Rachel, I think it was very gallant of him. That young man knows what he wants and he intends to get it. I think down deep you know what you want as well. Am I right?"

"I do love him."

"Then stop this nonsense."

"Aunt Mary—"

"Shush a minute and listen to me. You love Joshua. He loves you. It is as simple as that. Now, you need to make up your mind once and for all. Do you want to be happy with the man you love for the rest of your life, or do you intend to dally around with dandies at social events, never finding true love again?"

"But, Aunt Mary, I always thought you enjoyed the social scene as much as I did."

"I enjoy it, but that is because it is all I have. If I had a man like Joshua in love with me and I loved him too, nothing would stop me from being with him. I wouldn't care what he did for a living or where he lived. I would follow him anywhere. Think about that. And furthermore, I think a dominant man is just what the doctor ordered for you."

"Excuse me, please," Rachel said as she began to cry. She ran up the stairs to her room and shut the door, then threw herself on the bed.

She cried and kicked her legs until there were no more tears left. Exhausted, she got up and splashed her face with cold water. She fixed her hair and straightened her dress, then she sat down to think rationally.

Memories came flooding back to her. She remembered Joshua's kisses and how she had responded, especially the kiss today in her aunt's parlor. Her body had tingled all over and a wetness had seeped out between her legs. She had wanted more. More kisses, and touches, she had wanted him to touch her. Her nipples had grown taut beneath the fabric of her dress, as if they were begging for him to touch them. Yes, she knew what happened between a man and a woman, but she had never desired it until Joshua. Then she thought about the spanking he had given her after the incident at the social. Even though she had been shocked and embarrassed, a part of her had liked it, had liked that he cared enough to discipline her.

All this time, he had been a gentleman, going along with her aloofness. Until today. Today, he had shown her how he really felt. And surprisingly, she was not appalled by it. No, she had liked the way he had taken control, taken the decision, or indecision, out of her hands.

Her heart screamed, "Do it."

Her body achingly agreed, "Yes!"

Even her mind was now betraying her by saying, "It's time, Rachel."

So, she looked at herself in the mirror one last time and went downstairs to join her aunt and wait for Joshua's return.

"Are you feeling better, dear?" her aunt asked as she walked into the kitchen.

"Something smells good in here. Yes, I am fine now."

"I am making a roast for our supper. Be a dear and hand me that spoon so I can stir the vegetables."

"Here you go. Do I have time to bake a chocolate cake? It is one of Joshua's favorites."

Aunt Mary looked at her for a moment before saying, "Of course, dear. I should have all the ingredients. I didn't know you baked."

"Sarah taught me to make a chocolate cake, and everyone loves it, especially Joshua," she told her as she gathered the ingredients.

"Am I to assume this means you have come to a decision?" her aunt asked.

"I will marry Joshua," was all Rachel said in reply.

"Praise the Lord," Aunt Mary said. "About time you came to your senses. That is one handsome young man."

"I guess it's time to admit that everyone else was right and I was wrong. That's not an easy thing to do, and I have fought it for the longest time. But I am tired of fighting. I just want to be happy."

"Smart girl. I always said underneath your frivolous ways, you had a good head on your shoulders."

"Oh, Auntie, I am so sorry. Thank you so much for allowing me to come here and sort this all out."

"Well, sometimes it is a good thing to get away and have some time to think. Now, let's get this meal finished. Your husband-to-be will be back soon."

When supper was finished and the dishes done, Aunt Mary excused herself and went upstairs to her room, leaving the two young people alone to talk.

Rachel led Joshua to the parlor, where they sat on the lounge together. She took his hand, looked into his eyes, and said, "Joshua Thomas, if your offer still stands, I would be proud to be your wife."

He smiled. "I promise to make you very happy, Rachel." Then he leaned his face down to hers and kissed her.

All those sensations returned, the tingling, taut nipples, wetness, desire, heat. Rachel put her arms around his neck and played with the hair at his nape. She moved closer to him, giving him access. His hand moved to her breast and he cupped one fabric-covered mound in his hand.

"God, I want you, Rachel," he breathed as he moved his hand beneath her dress and underclothes to play with her nipple.

Rachel sighed. It felt so good. Why had she fought him for so long?

But then Joshua stopped. "Honey, we can't, not yet, not here. Let's get through the next few days, see my family, plan a small wedding first. I want to do this right. But first, there are some things we need to talk about. There are some things you don't know about me, and it's time I told you. Your family now knows. I told them before I came out here."

"Well, they must not be horrible if my father still gave you his blessing after you told him," she said.

"They are not horrible. In fact, I think you will be pleased. At least I hope so. I only hope you will understand why I did not tell you sooner."

"Now, I am curious. Please tell me," she said as she continued to run her fingers through his thick hair.

"You are a temptress. Do you know that? Settle down, so we can have a serious talk. And you have a spanking coming for that stunt you pulled. Running away and all."

"Yes, sir," she said demurely, shocking him. She placed her hands primly in her lap and said, "Go on. Tell me your deep, dark secrets."

"You remember that when we met, I had just come from my grandfather's funeral."

"Yes, and I couldn't believe you were going back to Oklahoma when you could have stayed here and worked in your family's business."

"Well, what I didn't tell you, didn't tell anyone, really, except a few people, was that I inherited a good deal of money from my grandfather. I invested part of it in Conrad's company, so he knew, of course, as did Sarah and Clyde, our driller." He waited for her reaction.

"So, that would mean you and Conrad are partners. That is why you went to the city on business with him and why you were in the office at times. But why were you working in the field? I don't understand."

"To learn the business from the ground up. Clyde kept telling me to tell you, but I wanted you to fall in love with *me*, not because I owned part of an oil company."

"Oh, Joshua, I am so sorry. I was so snooty, wasn't I?"

"Um, yes, you were. Clyde also said you needed your bottom tanned."

"He is Annabelle's husband, isn't he?" she asked with a giggle.

"He is. But there is more. With some more of the inheritance, I purchased a home. I hadn't moved into it yet as I stayed on at the bunkhouse until the current owner was able to move out."

"You own a house? I was wondering where we would live. Where is it?" she asked.

"I bought Mr. Ryan's house, next door to your parents' home. I bought it with the idea that you and I would live there together."

"That house sold shortly after we moved into ours. So that means—"

"That I knew from the first time we met I wanted to marry you," he finished for her.

"Oh, Joshua, I have been such a little fool. I did fall in love with you before I knew all that. But I wouldn't admit it to myself or anyone else. Since I got here, Aunt Mary has made me realize what I really wanted all along. Also, I met a man on the train. Don't worry, he was a perfect gentleman. He was an attorney, going to New York to begin a job there. I kept thinking he was the kind of man I was looking for, but something kept telling me he wasn't you. We took our meals together and talked, but nothing else. I just couldn't."

"You aren't angry with me?" he asked.

"No, how could I be? You always had my best interests at heart. I fought you all the way."

"I love you so much. And I am actually glad you met that man, even though you do make a habit of meeting men on trains." He chuckled. "But if it helped you to realize how you felt, it was a good thing for sure." He kissed her again then pulled back. "I should go. I can't guarantee that I can continue to be a gentleman around you for much longer. Just a few more days, and I will make you mine." He stood up and pulled her to her feet. "Walk me to the door?" he asked.

At the door, they kissed several more times before he finally left. He promised to pick her up after breakfast the next day to take her to meet his parents. It was a Saturday, so his father and brother would be at home.

The next morning at breakfast, she was nervous about the meeting.

"What's wrong?" her aunt asked.

"He is taking me to meet his family after breakfast."

"Just be yourself. That's all you need to do."

"But they were not happy with him the last time he saw them. How will they treat us?"

"He is their son. I would think they would be happy to hear that he is getting married. Do not fret so, dear. Just wait and see how things go."

Joshua picked her up and they arrived in front of a splendid old house in the better part of town. It wasn't too far from where her aunt lived. A butler answered the door and let them in. He led them to a large parlor and told them to have a seat.

"It's nice to see you again, Joshua. I will tell your parents you are here." He looked at Rachel and said, "Welcome, miss."

Soon, a handsome couple walked into the room, followed by a younger version of Joshua.

"Son, it's so good to see you. What brings you back?" his mother asked as she hugged him.

"Hey, brother, welcome home," his brother said.

"Son," his father said as he shook his hand.

"And who is this lovely creature?" his mother asked as she looked from her son to Rachel.

"Mom, Dad, Royce, this is my fiancée, Miss Rachel Linton. She is from Philadelphia but her family has relocated to Oklahoma. We met on the train out when I went back after Grandfather's funeral. She has been visiting her aunt here. I came out later, and we plan to marry before we go back home."

"Oh, how wonderful," his mother said as she gave Rachel a warm hug.

"Miss Linton, it is a pleasure to meet you," Mr. Thomas said.

"So my big brother is getting married," Royce said. "Who would have ever thought that would happen?"

"Sit, please, and tell us your plans," his mother said.

"As I said, we plan to marry here. I was hoping you would help Rachel and her aunt with the plans since her family won't be able to be here. They will hold a celebration for us when we return."

Rachel looked at him and then at his family. They were being very nice. Maybe things would be all right now.

"Of course, I will do what I can. It is short notice, but I am sure we can work something out. Perhaps you could hold the ceremony here, in the garden."

"Son, how are things in Oklahoma? Are you sure you want to go back?" his father asked.

"There are some things you don't know. Let me fill you in. I invested some money into an oil company. Appleby Oil, and my partner is married to Rachel's sister. I also bought a lovely house, next door to Rachel's parents. Things are going well. We struck oil on one of our sites recently."

"Maybe you could come to visit sometime," Rachel suggested.

"We would love to," Mrs. Thomas said.

"Son, I need to say some things to you as well. I was not happy when you decided to go back out west. I just couldn't understand. But I want you to know that I am proud of you. You went after your dream and didn't let me stand in your way. You stood up to me. Not many men would do that."

"Thank you, Dad," Joshua said as his dad shook his hand again.

"And then there is me, the younger son, who is nothing like his brother and wishes to follow in our father and grandfather's footsteps," Royce said.

"And there isn't anything wrong with that, as long as it is what you want, brother. I know you will do a good job and you will keep the family business going for a long time to come," Joshua said.

"Thanks, Josh."

"Excuse me for a moment. I have something for you, Joshua," his mother said.

A maid brought in tea for them. They were chatting amicably when Mrs. Thomas returned with a small box in her hand.

"Joshua, dear, this was my mother's. She asked that I keep it for you and give it to you when you brought your bride-to-be home. I am so happy you have chosen to include us in your plans." She handed the box to Joshua. Looking to her other son, she said, "And Grandmother Thomas' ring will go to you, Royce."

Joshua opened the box to reveal a solitary diamond set in a gold band. He looked at Rachel, then got down on one knee and placed it on her finger. "Now, it's official," he said.

"It's beautiful, and I am honored to wear your grandmother's ring." She looked at his mother. "Thank you. And I would like to get married in your garden."

"Will you stay for lunch? We can begin making plans," Mr. Thomas said.

"Of course," Rachel and Joshua both said.

They decided on a small wedding in the garden with only Aunt Mary, Mr. and Mrs. Thomas, and Royce and the girl he was currently courting in attendance. They did agree to a reception dinner at the Thomas' social club.

Aunt Mary and Rachel joined Mrs. Thomas on Tuesday to make the final preparations. The wedding was to be held on Saturday afternoon.

Joshua had immediately sent a wire to the family back in Oklahoma, informing them of the wedding and their plans to stay a few days before heading back.

Everything was ready on Saturday morning. As she was getting dressed in one of the bedrooms in the Thomas home, Aunt Mary told her she had a surprise for her.

"Oh, Auntie, you have already done so much," Rachel said.

"I think you will like this one, dear." Then the door opened and Rachel's mouth flew open as she saw her sister and mother enter the room.

"You are here! How?"

"Joshua sent a wire and we decided we had just enough time to get here. We arrived last night and stayed at the hotel so you wouldn't know. We wanted to surprise you," Sarah said.

"Your father and Conrad are with Joshua. Now, what can we do to help?" her mother asked.

"No tears!" Aunt Mary said. "Let's finish getting you ready."

The garden wedding was beautiful. Rachel enjoyed the reception at the social club, but she couldn't wait for it to be over. She and Joshua were going to stay at the hotel. Her family would move to Aunt Mary's where they would stay for a few days before returning home with the newlyweds. There was to be a party in Oklahoma when they returned.

"Who is taking care of the business?" Rachel asked Joshua at dinner.

"Clyde. Conrad and I will both be back soon. He will be able to handle it until then," he told her.

The couple said their goodbyes to their families and went to Joshua's hotel room to celebrate privately. Rachel thought she should have been anxious, but she wasn't. She couldn't wait to be in her new husband's arms.

At the door to their room, Joshua unlocked and opened the door, then scooped her up into his arms and carried her over the threshold and to the bed in the center of the room.

Rachel giggled.

"Are you happy, my love?" he asked.

"Very. And thank you for letting my family know in time to get here for the wedding. It was a nice surprise."

"You couldn't get married without them. They missed both of Sarah's weddings, so I knew they would want to be here for yours."

There was a bottle of champagne chilling on the table with two glasses. Joshua removed his jacket, took off his tie and rolled up his sleeves before opening it and filling the two glasses. He walked to the bed and handed one to her. "A toast to my beautiful, feisty bride." They clinked their glasses together and each took a sip.

"Now," he said as he took her glass and set it on the bedside table with his. "First things first. I told you that you have a punishment coming, so let's get that out of the way and then move on to the more pleasant things."

"Joshua! I was hoping you'd forgotten about that. I mean, everything worked out."

"Still, young lady, you gave us all a scare. I intend to start this marriage off the right way. And that means, you are going to be punished for your actions."

Without another word, he pulled her up from the bed and turned her around to remove her beautiful white lace gown. He unbuttoned the row of buttons in the back and pulled it over her shoulders. Rachel stepped out of it and Joshua laid it across a chair. Then he slowly removed her undergarments, sat down, and pulled her over his lap.

Rachel shivered, naked, about to be spanked. She couldn't say she was looking forward to it, yet she was excited in a way, too.

"My darling, you know why I am punishing you. Tell me why."

"B-because I left without telling anyone where I was going."

"Yes, and that is not a good thing to do, is it? A lot of people were concerned about your safety."

"I-I know, but—"

One sharp crack landed on her left cheek. Rachel jumped.

"I understand that you felt you needed to get away, for several reasons. No one is faulting you for that. You only needed to leave a note, and this could all have been avoided," Joshua said as his palm connected with her other cheek.

Several more smacks ensued, each one harder than the last, it seemed to Rachel. Although she was in great pain and her bottom felt like it was sizzling, there was another heat that ran through her entire body, waking up every nerve ending.

She was leaking fluid onto his trousers, she knew, and she was embarrassed. Would he notice? Her nipples were standing at attention, aching to be touched. She felt a yearning deep inside that needed to be fulfilled, but she had yet to experience what, exactly, would help it.

Her entire body ached. Her bottom felt like it had been

burned with hot coals, and the rest of her felt like it needed to be doused with cold water.

Still, Joshua's hard hand continued to rain down smacks on her already cherry red bottom. Finally, he stopped and pulled her to a sitting position on his lap.

"Oh, it hurts!" she said as she hid her face in his shirt and let the tears fall.

"I know, baby, I know. But all is forgiven now. I am going to lay you down on the bed and I will rub some liniment on that sore behind of yours. All right? I will be right back."

He laid her gently on her stomach then went to the water closet to retrieve the liniment he had promised. When he came back, he lovingly rubbed it over her sore bottom as he said sweet words to her in a low voice.

The liniment did make her feel better as it cooled some of the heat she had felt. But the other heat, the one inside her body, was not going to go away until it was appeased.

"Joshua?" she asked timidly.

"Yes, sweetheart?"

"M-make love to m-me. Please."

"I would love nothing better." He lay down beside her and began to kiss her neck as he took the pins from her hair and let it flow freely then pushed it to the side. Then he very carefully rolled her to her back before giving each nipple his attention.

Rachel sighed. It felt heavenly, but it was also making that inferno inside her hotter and more out of control.

She arched her hips instinctively, and Joshua chuckled. "Slow down, feisty girl. We'll get there."

He continued to lavish her with kisses, moving from her breasts to her flat stomach, and on down her legs. He kissed down one and up the other until he came to that special place between her legs. Suddenly, Rachel felt embarrassed. She knew she was wet down there. Surely, he wouldn't... But that was exactly what he did. He kissed her there and she nearly flew off the bed, it felt so divine. Then he used his tongue on her, finding a spot that must have been really special, because it made her want him all the more. She needed him inside her. She knew that was how it worked, so why wasn't he doing it? He still had his clothes on, for goodness' sake.

Still following his lead, she waited to see what he would do next. He inserted a finger inside her and it felt so good. He began to pump and he said, "I need to get you ready for me, sweetheart. It's going to hurt the first time I enter you, but this should help prepare you. And after that first time, it will feel good. I promise."

She nodded and he added another finger. Soon, she felt as if she was climbing a mountain and she needed to reach the top. Up, and up, and up, she went until finally, she reached the crest and wave after wave of sensations filled her. She shuddered and Joshua held her close. When she finally recovered, he got up and quickly removed his clothes.

He stood next to the bed for her to look at him. Then he took his hard member in his hand and said, "I don't know how much you know about how this all works, but this is what I will put inside you."

"I-I know the mechanics of it, but how in the world?"

Joshua chuckled. "Oh, darling, it will work, believe me. You probably have felt yourself getting wet down there. Well, that is your body preparing you for me. And those feelings you experienced a few minutes ago will be even stronger when I am inside you."

"Show me," she said as she beckoned for him to join her again.

"Um, gladly," he murmured as he lay beside her. He kissed her and then started an exploration of her body again, getting her ready for penetration. Finally, when he could wait no longer and he thought she was as ready as she would be, he moved over so that he was atop her. He kissed her again and then nudged her opening with the tip of his penis.

"Now, sweetheart, I am going to go inside you very slowly at first. Once I've pierced your maidenhead and the pain subsides, I will show you more pleasure. Are you ready?"

Rachel nodded again, slightly apprehensive but also curious.

Joshua penetrated her as he said, slowly, until he felt her barrier give way to him. He stopped and looked at her face to gage her reaction. "Are you all right?" he asked.

"Yes, it burned but is getting better."

Still moving slowly, he kept going until he was completely inside her. Stopping again, he said, "Now, I am going to start moving harder and faster inside you. Move your hips in rhythm with my thrusts. Can you do that?"

"Y-yes," she said. She arched her hips as he thrust once, hard. Then he continued to move inside her until she caught on to the pace, and they moved together.

That inferno was building inside her again as he had said it would. She was climbing the mountain for a second time, only this time, it was with more urgency. It felt so good, now that the burning had stopped. And when she reached the top, she cried out his name, "Joshua!" He joined her at the top and after a while, they came down together. They lay quietly for a few minutes and then he got up and went to the water closet. When he came out, he was carrying a washrag and towel. He carefully cleaned her up with the warm cloth.

"Now, I do not want you to be alarmed, but you will see a bit of blood on the sheet and the cloth. That is normal for your first time. It's all right, nothing to be concerned about," he said as he dried her with the towel.

"Oh, I am so embarrassed. What will the staff think when they come in to clean?" she asked.

"I think they have seen it before and will not think a thing about it, feisty girl." He handed her the glass of champagne.

She sat up and sipped the bubbly drink. "Joshua?" she asked.

"Yes?"

"Was I… all right? I mean, did I do it right?"

"Oh, sweetheart, you were perfect. Now, why don't you get some rest? It's been a busy several days."

"Can we do that again soon?"

"Anytime you want. Now sleep. I'll be right here with you."

And they did it again several times before they met the rest of the family to head back out west. They said goodbye to his family, who promised to visit soon, and then they were on their way to the train station.

The party of six boarded the train for home. Several days later, they were back in Oklahoma. Conrad and Joshua had work to catch up on, leaving Rachel free to become accustomed to being a wife. She took great joy in working on the house, even though her mother and sister had done a wonderful job of making it a home for her and Joshua. She returned to the library a few days a week, which made Mrs. Richards very happy. The first Sunday they were home, there was a celebration at the church for the newlyweds after the service. Many of their friends were in attendance. She even saw the girl she had spotted around town a few times, but she was with a different man this time. Rachel wondered who she was and what her story was. Maybe she would find out, but today, she was too busy accepting well wishes from several people she knew.

And each evening, after supper, she and Joshua found pleasure in each other's arms.

About a month later, she was just finishing up some chores when there was a knock on the door. She set her dishtowel on the counter and walked out of the kitchen to answer it.

She was surprised to see her mother and Aunt Mary standing on her doorstep. Her mother came over frequently, as did Sarah, but she certainly wasn't expecting to see her aunt again so soon.

"Come on in. I'll make some tea. Aunt Mary, what on earth are you doing here?"

She busied herself making tea and cutting slices of apple cake while the women sat down in her cheery kitchen. Sarah had been giving her more lessons in baking.

"Your home is beautiful, Rachel," Aunt Mary said.

"Thank you. Mother and Sarah got it ready for us, and I have been adding a few touches here and there," she said as she served the cake and tea and sat down to join them. "Now, you didn't answer my question. What on earth brings you out west?"

"You look very happy, dear. And really, that is what brings me here. Having you with me for those few days and talking to you made me realize I am wasting my life in Philadelphia. My family is here. I have nothing keeping me there, no love interest. Friends, yes, but I can make new ones. I spoke to George and Rosella when they stayed with me after the wedding, and I decided to sell my house and come here. I can always go back if I don't adjust. My house is sold, and here I am. I will be staying next door with your parents for a while, while I look for a small house, but I am in no hurry, and they have assured me they want me for as long as I'll stay. They don't even want me to find a house, but eventually, I will."

"That's right. We are happy to have her with us. It is so quiet since you moved out, Rachel. Even though you are right next door, we don't want to intrude on you and Joshua, nor do we wish to bother Sarah and Conrad. So having Mary here will be great fun. I can introduce her to all the ladies at the church and help her get settled in before she finds a place of her own," Rachel's mother said. "This cake is delicious."

"Thank you. Sarah has been giving me baking and cooking lessons. Now, Aunt Mary, are you sure about this?" She turned her attention back to her beloved aunt.

"Oh, yes, very sure, my dear. And your mother is right about the cake."

What a strange turn of events. Here, I wanted to go back to Aunt Mary, but instead, she is here with us. It will be wonderful having her close again, Rachel thought as she looked from her mother to her aunt and smiled.

"Who knows? I may be like you and find the man of my dreams here," Aunt Mary said.

CHAPTER 16

AMY

$\mathcal{E}$vidently Amy's plans changed. For many reasons, thankfully. She accepted Mr. Ramsey's Thursday dinner invitation. She offered to return to work on Saturday. And Ruth had a fella.

The initial idea of riding to Glen's with Ruth and bunking in her room for the night before catching the Saturday train headed east required reassessment. Not only because she didn't wish to intrude on her friend, but somehow, apparently, she meant to stay. Well, she needed a place to stay. Not a hotel room or inconveniencing a friend but to find an individual or couple renting a room until she figured it all out. She would not dwindle her funds on an expensive room at the hotel after Friday. Returning to the front desk, she informed Iva she would definitely require the use of the room the following evening, and maybe longer.

Enlisting Ruth to travel to Glen Jernigan's home and burial

site might have been the smartest and most beneficial decision she made. Beneficial to many, but selfish as well.

He had lived in a tiny, one room shack. Tidy. But isolated. She hated herself for thinking it, but she would not have been satisfied there. She craved social interaction. She appreciated opportunities to contribute to a community. They would have made it work. And nevertheless, he deserved to be recognized and honored.

Ruth recited scripture. Amy sang a hymn. Neither spoke a word for at least an hour after they left.

"Where do you go from here?" Ruth asked, breaking their comfortable silence.

"To the Beecher property." Amy suppressed her laughter. The shock on Ruth's face over the inconceivable suggestion of them voluntarily summoning any attention from the Beecher brothers reduced them to hysterics.

Gasping and hugging her abdomen, Ruth questioned, "And why would any respectable female visit them?"

Overcome again by the absurdity of her directive, Amy explained, "My dear friend, Josie, is there. I can't forget her. No good soul should ever be forgotten."

Jerking the reins to encourage the horse to pick up the pace, Ruth empathized, "It's good. We will go. Only because it is on our way back into town. And we can't stay long. As in… I won't leave without you."

No words were needed. The horse trotted along, and the beauty of the surrounding landscape stunned her. She never truly regarded it, so she never truly appreciated it. It differed from Virginia and still offered beauty.

Directing the horse and wagon off the primary thoroughfare, they rode into raw and unmanaged land pitted with prairie dog holes. She glimpsed a dwelling in the distance, but in order to reach it, they entered a section laden with thorny brush.

Chickens ran amok. Pigs snorted and ran in the dense, over-grown thicket.

Amy's trepidation and aversion disappeared in the wake of Josie's nearby, definitive warning, "Amos, if you don't repair that chicken coop and mend the hog fence by dinner... you will leave the house for the evening and lose your watching while I bathe privileges."

Ignoring Ruth's appalled glare, Amy became emotional seeing her small redheaded friend ahead of them on a porch wielding a broom and commanding all around her. An irre-pressible fit of laughter overcame her. That little, fiery, disrep-utable woman possessed Amy's heart. As did Lizzie. As did Jose. And she refused to apologize for her heart any longer. She loved. She loved unconditionally and hard.

"Amy... is that you I see sneaking onto our property. Get on over here and have a whiskey with me." Josie dropped the broom, dashed over and jumped on the wagon. She threw an arm around Amy's neck.

"I wasn't sneaking. Just confirming you are safe and happy," Amy explained.

"Very. We have this little piece of crap property. But I am using my power of persuasion to get these boys to make it more suitable for a lady. I've got five men who bombard me with... a multitude of things." Josie winked and smirked. "Jeb and I are marrying Monday. That should appease the 'judgmental'. Then I plan to reintroduce the family to the community. We will attend Sunday services." Leaping to the ground, she waved toward the porch. "Come on ladies. Boys, get three glasses and the good whiskey. Not that homemade crap you call whiskey."

The Beecher boys, big and intimidating men, scurried inside the home and brought out chairs and delivered glasses and poured drinks. "I'm sorry I left without any word. I couldn't think straight when Naomi and Nathan showed up at the stable and fetched Lola. The situation forced me to act on my indecision about bailing out Jeb and Amos. And, in choosing to live the life I desired with five men in whatever capacity we agree and enjoy."

They sat and drank and discussed the events that brought them to their current situations. At least Amy and Josie did. Ruth listened and enjoyed the whiskey. Josie seemed happy. She asked about Jose, but Amy deflected, "I can't answer. Last night I planned to leave for Virginia. Today, I know I am staying here in Oklahoma."

Josie whined for them not to leave when they announced their departure. "Don't be a stranger. If you don't attend the Sunday service, I will come to the restaurant. I know you will never snub me," Josie stated, but her eyes yearned for affirmation.

"I'm excited for our next visit." Amy waved and smiled as they exited the decrepit property. She had reconnected with Josie, a woman she befriended at the Parlor. A woman residing with the criminal Beecher brothers. She had a friend. A friend supported a friend unless it unjustly or selfishly hurt another. Josie hadn't hurt anyone.

"I'm proud of you," Ruth declared as the horse dug its hooves into dry ground and the wagon jutted forward.

Amy couldn't imagine what for. She dreaded delving into it. It might free emotions she fought to manage since they headed out that morning.

"I like Josie. Did she come here as a mail order bride too? She is lucky to have you. You were dealt a lousy hand, but you haven't folded. And you still put others above yourself. The only reason I could go with you today is because we hired a couple of the Gonzales women. They are hardworking and my workload has diminished because of them." She sighed and relaxed with an enviable blissful expression across her face. "I don't know what to do with myself with the extra time on my hands."

Amy suspected Ruth resolved a portion of that issue with

taking up more time with a man. "Be happy. This is time you can use to claim your happiness." After speaking the recommendation, the advice she gave resonated with Amy. Both women should practice what they preached.

~

ANY CONCERNS over keeping herself busy until she trusted her decisions were snuffed Saturday in the restaurant. The tables stayed occupied, and they had customers waiting. The relief she experienced when she and Ruth returned to the hotel and Iva pulled her aside to speak to her quickly transformed into regret.

Jose had come earlier. Iva described his demeanor as forlorn. He asked if Amy left word for him but appeared unaffected when told she had not.

"I hope I haven't made a grave error in my judgement, but I told him you were out and had rented your room tonight and indefinitely. He brightened in front of my very eyes hearing it."

Flinging her arms around Iva's shoulders, Amy gushed, "I'm happy you did." Good golly was she. In a matter of a minute, she bounced from pure joy over learning he came to utter despair over hurting him and back to elation that Iva informed him she intended to stay, and it pleased him.

Don't be rash. Be confident in your decisions. She loved Jose. She could waste precious time mourning what might have been and never would with Glen. Or she could seize the love and devotion she had with Jose. But she couldn't rush it.

She had friends still. She enjoyed working again. Risking her relationship with Jose was not an option. She couldn't become overzealous.

Sunday, she attended the church service. Mrs. Wilson asked if she wanted to and offered to work in the morning if she handled the afternoon and dinner shift. The fear of being shunned by the locals still unsettled her. But no time like the present to begin the process of inserting herself in the community. The longer she delayed, the harder it might become. So, she accepted. Possibly Josie would come.

Another wise decision. Not only did Josie show with all five of the Beecher brothers clean and dressed appropriately for church, but Mr. O'Brien stood with the choir behind the pulpit in an obvious frenzy. His arms flitted about as he issued instructions. Wiping sweat from his brow with the back of his hand, he turned toward the congregation and displayed a face the color of a plum. The moment his eyes caught sight of her, he charged her. "Amy, I'm the choir director, and our lead soprano isn't here because of a sick child, and she had a solo."

Remaining as inconspicuous as she could resulted in failure. He, as had Mr. Ramsey, behaved as any casual acquaintance would. And what a relief. The fact they met at the Parlor didn't faze him. And being that he directed the church choir, that fact she trusted would remain their secret. "I'm sorry, Mr. O'Brien." She glanced around to confirm she hadn't misjudged their interaction. She observed men shaking hands, women hugging one another. All oblivious to the exchange between her and Mr. O'Brien.

"I beg you to sing in her place," he expressed. Lowering his voice to merely a whisper, he praised, "You have such a beautiful voice. What better place to share it than in God's house?"

Should she? Could she? Yes. She came to worship their Lord. She came to socialize with others doing the same.

Once she agreed, he ushered her to the front and introduced her to the other members. He handed her a hymn book and gave her the titles. The other members were excited to meet her and thrilled she joined them.

Her hands trembled as she watched Laura Garrison with her baby in her arms, Irving and Marian Slater, Lizzie and Floyd, and many unfamiliar faces funnel into the front pews. Once they noticed her, they smiled and waved. Lizzie teared up and blew her a kiss.

Taking a seat at the piano, Mr. O'Brien began to play, and she immersed herself in the melody, the words, and the riveting spirituality. Finishing the second song and moving to sit as the pastor stepped up to begin his sermon, enthusiastic clapping gave everyone pause.

Jose. He evidently slipped in during their performance and took a place behind Lizzie and Floyd. He stood, clapping his hands together. It embarrassed her. It exhilarated her.

The pastor clapped too. "That, young man, is an inspiration. Rejoice in the power of our Lord and welcome his glory into your hearts."

If she tried, she couldn't stop from welcoming it all. Jose worshipped his form of religion at services on the farm. Yet, he stood and celebrated at hers. For her.

The sermon garnered a multitude of 'Amens'. The pastor delivered the final prayer, and the people began exiting the church. Lizzie and Laura waited for her and hugged her and expressed their gladness to see her again. Squirming in her mother's arms and fighting to be free of them, Laura's baby fussed. "I am taking her outside. I will see you out there," she grunted. "This child inherited both mine and Everett's tenacity."

Lizzie stammered, "I-I'm just so damn ecstatic you didn't leave." Tugging Amy's hand, she pulled her into a pew. "I am mortified over my confused impulses. And I am ashamed I enlisted your aid." She lowered her head and tilted it away from Amy. She sniffled. "To know you don't harbor any contempt for me is a blessing beyond what I deserve."

"I, too, have erred. We can't judge one another. Our heavenly Father is burdened with that task." She took Lizzie's hand. "You and I will always be friends. We are imperfect. As we were designed."

Did she really say that? She couldn't have. Since when did she speak hard yet undisputable truths. It originated with Lizzie. Lizzie's doubts about Glen... Nathan. Lizzie's dilemma. Both women suffered. Both sustained.

"Floyd is building an addition to the house for the baby. Mr. Slater is thinking about relocating from Oklahoma City to here. He wishes to be involved in the child's life. I am blessed."

"Yes. You are," Amy agreed. Where had Jose gone? Maybe he waited outside too.

"Promise me you will come visit. You will love it. The acreage we reside on is near all my family from Texas. They farm and I can show you the orchards I started. They are abundant with fruit. I am proud of them. Except I can't keep the kids from sneaking in there and plucking fruit before they're fully ripe." Lizzie pumped Amy's hand a few times before releasing it and standing. "I've retained you long enough. Please continue singing. Here, anywhere. You do it magnificently."

They were the last two to leave the church. Floyd approached immediately. Laura brought several people over and introduced them to her. Not that she would ever remember. She didn't see Jose. She focused on him. Or the absence of him. She scanned the crowd. She wondered where he went. She wavered on broaching it to Lizzie.

Beyond the gathering, Naomi stepped out from under the shade of a tree. She started for Amy, but Mr. Slater approached her, and they conversed. All the while her eyes remained on Amy. It made it difficult for her to concentrate on anything other than their looming encounter. If she could excuse herself and depart the scene, she could avoid it. It gave her a sense of unease and imminent regress. She would put it behind her and eventually forgive Naomi and Nathan, but it hadn't been nearly long enough.

More and more people came and introduced themselves. She recalled their names, not their faces. Emma. Claude. Annabelle.

Clyde. Clara Mae. Clayton. And the overexcited activity of the children nearby squealing and laughing overwhelmed her.

"I apologize for intruding, but I wish to speak with Amy," Josie declared coming up behind her and linking their arms. She guided her away from the never-ending stream of strangers. "You appear somewhat as a trapped animal needing rescue." She chuckled.

Breathing in and out of her nose, she waited until her heart slowed. "I'm glad you are my hero."

Josie nudged her shoulder with hers. "Look at those boys. I swear... will I ever train them enough to risk bringing them out?"

The five Beecher brothers were at a wagon in poor condition. Two of them were on the ground wrestling. One tugged at the collar of his shirt. Another kicked rocks into the crowd. The fifth held his hat in front of him and gazed lovingly at Josie.

"Never a dull moment with this bunch. I'm proud of my Jeb, though. Look at him. He could pass for a true gentleman." She gestured him over and he raced to her. "Take control of your brothers before I make a scene none of you will likely forget anytime soon." He hurried away to do her bidding.

"Please, may I have a word?" Naomi surprised both women. Remaining several feet away, hesitantly awaiting approval before further approaching, she peered at them. As pretty as she looked, she had no air of confidence and kept her chin down. Reaching into her purse, she retrieved a bulk of cash and offered it to Amy. "This is what Nathan took from you. I also included funds Mr. Slater requested I give you."

Whoa. What an unexpected turn of events. A peace offering? She accepted the money but didn't comment.

"I pray one day you forgive us. It seems we are remaining in the area. The Pendergrasses are wonderful people and are becoming like family to us. Mr. Slater is sponsoring a lifetime dream of mine... to manage and perform in a playhouse. A reputable one which we hope will offer entertainment to the many people who pass through. I would be honored if you would consider participating." She sighed and visibly swallowed before meeting Amy's eyes. "You have natural talent. Your strong, lovely voice would be a wonderful gain for it. Anyway, Nathan and I came for the service, but once we saw you standing with the choir, we decided to not attend. I had him go and fetch the money and I waited outside for you. We want to mend fences, not cause you additional turmoil."

Amy nodded. "I appreciate it." Contemplating anything beyond that confounded her.

"Amos!" Josie shouted, terminating the awkward exchange. She fisted her hand and shook it in the air at him.

"I hope to see you around." Naomi smiled and fled to join an older couple standing with Irving and Marian Slater, presumably the Pendergrasses. The woman slid her arm around Naomi's waist and pulled her into her side.

Josie grumbled, "Give me a hug. I'm gonna go cuff Amos upside his idiot head and get them away from civilized people before they ruin our acceptance forever."

They embraced and Amy watched her march to the wagon. And did she ever deliver a blow to his jaw. It made her smile. Little Josie ruled a bunch of overgrown boys. Naomi and Nathan making amends. Things were beginning to fall into place and feel right. All except for being with Jose again.

Before anyone else could command her attention, she started the walk back into town and to the hotel. Reaching the bank, she noticed Jose leaning into a railing up ahead. He had his arms crossed in front of his chest and his legs crossed at the ankles. Casual and comfortable. He grinned at her and her legs trembled. Her heart quit beating before resuming in a galloping rate. Oh, how he affected her.

She yearned to run to him and into his arms but practiced self-restraint instead. He straightened and stood gazing at her in a profound love she returned. This dignified, alluring gentleman loved her. And she him.

"I assume the enormous smile across your stunning face is for me," he greeted.

Without question. Being in his presence made a bright day brighter. She missed him beyond belief. The closer she came to him, the less she cared about propriety. She opened her arms and hurried to him. Barely flinging his open to catch her as she jumped at him, he lifted her off her feet and hugged her firmly to him. His head beside hers, he whispered, "I have been miserable without you."

IT HAD BEEN three weeks since Amy doubted if she would ever be happy again. And what a whirlwind few weeks it had been. How had she ever considered leaving Oklahoma and Jose behind? Women dream of having a man and a love like what she had with Jose. And in less than an hour, she and Jose would be husband and wife.

Josie stuck a hairpin in her scalp. "Ouch, why did you do that?" Amy whined.

"Because I've been talking to you, and you are glassy-eyed and not responding." Josie did it again for emphasis. "Do I have your attention now?"

Shoving her elbow into Josie's ribs, she remarked, "Well, you do now. But there are kinder ways to gain it." She sat in front of the mirror with Josie standing behind her and arranging her hair for the ceremony. It reflected the image of her friend sticking her tongue out.

"I know it is your day and all, but I was telling you about Mr. Pendergrass hiring Jeb as a farmhand. I'm so proud of him. He looks so dashing today. It makes me want to lure him away from the guests, undress him, and—"

"Josie, shh," scolded Amy.

The door opened and Annabelle hurried in with the wedding dress draped over her arms. "I'm sorry. So sorry I'm late. I made a few last-minute adjustments and I think you'll love them," she explained, laying the garment on the bed.

Lizzie knocked on the door before entering. "Don't leave me out. I can't wait to see you all dressed."

Bouncing out of the chair, she viewed the gown for the first time. She had never seen anything as beautiful. Annabelle took the simple, plain white dress Amy gave her and adorned it with lace. She sewed lace at the collar, the hem, and at the wrists. And the pearls. Where had she acquired all the pearls embellishing the bodice?

"Mr. Ramsey insisted I use a string of pearls which belonged to his mother and one his wife left behind," Annabelle said.

Raising her eyes to the ceiling, Amy couldn't prevent the tears from forming and seeping then. Jose invited Mr. Ramsey and Mr. O'Brien. And the compassion and tolerance he demonstrated in doing it warmed her heart until it must have melted.

The ceremony went fast. But the celebration didn't. The amount of food they served, and the music and dancing impressed her. They married on the Gonzales' farm. Jose and his family built them a small cabin down from and out of view of Floyd and Lizzie's, alongside the creek. There were many tears shed that day. Jose's family welcomed her into their large, vivacious group. She would never want for anything. She had the man of her dreams and a beautiful life.

Alone at last in their new home, Jose led her to the bedroom. Since the day he waited for her outside the bank, he took exorbitant measures to ensure they were never alone. On Sundays, he had Lizzie escort her to and from the church service. When he arranged to have her come to the farm for a visit with him and his family, he had Diego bring her and return her to the hotel. Iva Whitfield gave her a reduced rate because she worked at the restaurant, which allowed her to stay there until the wedding. And as much as she yearned to touch and kiss and continue where she and Jose left off in her hotel room after he spanked her, she respected and appreciated his determination. She didn't possess the strength to deny him... well, herself.

"Mrs. Gonzales, I apologize if my assumptions are incorrect, and if I am speaking inconsiderately and crudely, but if you and I are not undressed and in the bed within the next minute I swear I might either die or behave offensively."

She laughed. "I concur with your suggestion whole-heartedly."

A commotion ensued of hands and fingers and buttons and garments. Naked before one another, Jose admired her body. She experienced no shame or modesty. He turned her around and removed the remaining pins from her hair before circling her back to face him. Combing his fingers through her hair, he professed, "I am the luckiest man to ever live. You are stunning."

She believed it when he touched her and gazed at her. She knew he would protect her. She trusted him implicitly. "And you are striking and incite a surge of love and lust within me," she confessed. But could it be labeled a confession? She offered herself to him weeks ago. The darker coloring of his skin mesmerized her. She admired the hair on his masculine chest and reached out and rubbed her fingertips over it. As much as she craved the intimacy in becoming one with him during the sexual act, she had yet to brave dropping her eyes any lower.

Slipping his hand over hers, he directed her to the bed. He guided her onto it. Kissing her neck, her shoulder, between her breasts and down to her stomach, he took an ankle in each hand and bent and splayed her legs.

Before she had a chance to voice her opposition, he planted his face in between her bared thighs. Her knees involuntarily tensed and gripped his neck.

"Release me. And relax," he coaxed.

She did as he suggested, and his heated breath stimulated her in deplorable regions and extracted detestable responses. Her mind emptied as her body's pleasure and responses consumed her. As indecent as it was—she hoped it never ended. He exhaled on her thighs and kissed them. He blew over her never exposed or touched private region. The bursts and puffs he distributed rendered her a captive to him and his control over her body.

The contact of something other than air surprised her. Realizing he used his tongue stunned her. "Jose, this..." she moaned. Oh... anyone, everyone please forgive her. She hated it. She craved it. She begged him to stop. She begged him to never stop. He placed his tongue and flicked it until she couldn't decipher right from wrong. All she knew was it couldn't end.

He clutched her thighs, holding them open and available. He swiped his tongue low then upward. He circled it over the top. He sucked on her. Her legs quivered. "If you feel naughty after this and need a spanking, I am happy to oblige. And I will be the only one to ever oblige," he emphasized in a throaty warning.

Lifting her hands, she grasped his head and pressed his face against her, encouraging him to maintain the euphoria he gifted her and to somehow relieve her of her blissful discomfort. Her core constricted and pulsated. She closed her eyes tightly and her body jerked as wave after wave of a heavenly frenzy assaulted her.

Whimpers escaped her throat as she descended. "Will it always be like this?" she murmured.

Still with his face in between her thighs, he chuckled. "I promise it will."

Digging his elbows into the mattress, he scooted up and above her. Their eyes met and held. She raised her hands to his face and caressed it. "I love you, Jose."

He kissed her deeply and meaningfully. No other response required... besides the one he gave her in the kiss. He worshipped her mouth with his lips and his tongue. And soon enough, her center tautened, and she slid her feet up the back of his calves.

"I love you, Amy Gonzales. If anyone dares deceive you or harm you in any manner again… they will regret it. This may hurt, but I will do the best I can." He brushed his lips over hers and positioned himself at her entrance. He thrust. She winced. He planted kisses on her forehead. "You are breached. You will suffer soreness, but it will only get better."

Clamping her fingers on his hips, she prompted him to resume. Having him inside her provided everything she required and desired. He began a methodical motion of gliding in and out of her until they both lost themselves to the rhythm. Both shook and gasped and moaned until they existed together in perfect rapture.

ISABELLA KOLE

USA Today and International bestselling author, Isabella Kole, lives in southern Indiana, where she enjoys spending time with her family and friends. Always an avid romance reader, she began writing several years ago, and although she has had several sweet romances published under a different pen name, Accepting His Terms is the first erotic romance in her collection. When not writing, Isabella can be found traveling around signing books and meeting her readers or simply enjoying life.

You can find Isabella on Facebook at: https://www.facebook.com/pages/Isabella-Kole-Author/ and at Amazon: http://www.amazon.com/Isabella-Kole/

Don't miss these exciting titles by Isabella Kole and Blushing Books!

Josie's Seasons
Rebecca and the Rancher
Hannah's Horror
The Seduction of E.J.
The Highlander's Curse
The Marshall and the Heiress
Rescuing Raven
Her Captain's Command
The Daring Doms
In the Palm of His Hand

Big G Ranch Series (with Sheri Lynn)

Resisting the Ranchers
Romancing the Ranchers
Respecting the Roughnecks
Redeeming the Roughnecks

Avalon Adventure Series
The Academy
Karia and the Prince

Dominant Men Series
Her Blue Collar Dom
Her Convenient Dom
Her Promised Dom
Her Texas Dom
Her Second-Chance Dom
Her Hesitant Dom
Her Ambitious Dom

Desire for Discipline Series
Accepting His Terms, Book One
Submitting to Brian, Book Two
The Longing Within, Book Three
Desire for Discipline Collection

Loving the Nobleman Series
Remington's Rules, Book One
Emily's Emergence, Book Two
Duchess's Desire, Book Three

Submitting to Her Professor - With Coleen Singer

Anthologies
Modern Day Doms Collection
His Rules Collection

12 Naughty Days of Christmas, 2015

Audiobooks
The Daring Doms
In the Palm of His Hand
Hannah's Horror
Her Captain's Command
Emily's Emergence
Duchess's Desire
Remington's Rules
The Marshal and the Heiress
Rescuing Raven
The Seduction of E.J.

SHERI LYNN

Sheri Lynn was an Army brat, so her childhood involved moving every three years. However, truly a southern gal, she currently resides in Alabama with her husband, two Chihuahuas, a mean cat, turtle, and a teenage daughter. She also has two sons, who live on their own, and a stepson and stepdaughter.

Romance novels have always been her reading choice. She is a hopeless romantic, and that trait materializes in every aspect of her life. "Wearing your heart on your sleeve" has been a common phrase repeatedly heard in her life. Writing romance and 'happily ever after's comes naturally.

Whether a result of her childhood or not, she loves to travel. Warm weather and beautiful beaches are always her choice destination.

Don't miss these exciting titles from Blushing Books and Sheri Lynn!

Rekindling Ash

Big G Ranch Series (with Isabella Kole)
Resisting the Ranchers
Romancing the Ranchers
Respecting the Roughnecks
Redeeming the Roughnecks

The Heart Facts
The Heart Won't Forget, Book 1

The Heart Will Lead, Book 2

Heroines of Neoma Series
Charm Him, Disarm Him, Book 1

Eternal Gifts Series
His Eternal Promise, Book 1

Anthologies
12 Naughty Days of Christmas 2016

Contact Sheri Lynn:
sherilynnauthor@yahoo.com

BLUSHING BOOKS

Blushing Books is the oldest eBook publisher on the web. We've been running websites that publish steamy romance and erotica since 1999, and we have been selling eBooks since 2003. We have free and promotional offerings that change weekly, so please do visit us at http://www.blushingbooks.com/free.

BLUSHING BOOKS NEWSLETTER

Please join the Blushing Books newsletter
to receive updates & special promotional offers.
You can also join by using your mobile phone:
Just text BLUSHING to 22828.

Every month, one new sign up via text messaging will receive a
$25.00 Amazon gift card, so sign up today!